Blind Beauty

Lexy Paullin

Contents

Chapter 1- Darkness

E vangeline's PovDarkness. That's all I see. It's always been like this, seeing nothing not knowing what colors are or letters or anything. I've always wanted to know what a dog looks like. I have one, her name is one of the only words I know semi what it looks like because when I felt it I called her Lily. Because I love flowers and how they smell.

"Evangeline! Are you ready to get your clothes on?" My mom asked from downstairs, I yelled back a yes and she sent my boyfriend, Jake Micheals. He has been here since day one even after years of being together he's been here. Mom trust him to help me around and everything cause he and my mom are literally best friends. He always calls my parents by their names, Ben and Natasha. I heard my door open and I still kept my head in the position it was in. I mean what's the point to even look.

"Let's get you dressed" Jake said coming over to me helping me up and to my closet. He took off my pajamas and put on my clothes.

"What am I wearing today?" I asked while he patted down my clothes and brushed my hair into a ponytail.

"Your wearing a teal dress with pink flowers on the end of it with pink flats" he said finishing my ponytail and kissing my cheek. I smiled and he helped me up taking me out of my room downstairs to where my mom, dad, and sister Sam is.

"Hello sweetheart" my dad said kissing the top of my head taking me away from Jake to sit down. When I did I heard a clink in front of me indicating my mom sat down a plate of food for me. I felt a hand wrap around my shoulder and pull me into them and I knew instantly that it was my mother.

"Good morning sweetie! Enjoy your breakfast"

"Thanks mom" I said while she said you're welcome to me. Jake sat next to me feeding me eggs and bacon with toast. After I was done he helped me up and took me out grabbing his pack back and mine while Sam followed us. We drove to our school and he helped me out and I could already tell you people are probably looking at me.

"Hey. It'll be ok Eve" Sam said using her nickname she made for me I smiled and nodded my head. Sam and Jake are my only friends. I can tell you who the cool kids are, they are the coolest kids in school but they're nice. It's Max, Devon, Xan, and their leader Edrick. I've never really talked or even heard from Edrick. I accidentally bumped into Max and Devon once when I tried to walk by myself they helped me pick my stuff up and then Xan came and took me to my classroom handing me back over to Jake who was upset I tried to walk by myself. I talked a little to them but not much.

"We're here Evangeline" Jake said I nodded thanking him while he walked me in and sat me down while he sat next to me. He is in every one of my classes because he always helps me. I have reading first which is hard for me. And I always have A's and it's hard to tell Jake my answers when people always like to copy off of me. Jake doesn't though, he does his test before me and then helps me.

"So today we will be learning about.." our teacher talked and talked about sentences and everything. I told what things to copy down for Jake to write down and told him to point these things out and everything. Soon the bell rung and our teacher told us one last thing that I was smirking about.

"I hope you all took notes because there is going to be a quiz tomorrow over everything you've learned today" and by the teachers tone he was smirking, me and Jake chuckled as the rest of the class groaned as we got up. Being a senior is hard especially being a blind senior but I make it, my classmates just don't care and that's why they don't make good grades. Soon it was lunch time and Jake told me what we were having today which is hot dogs or burgers. I told him what I wanted we paid and sat down outside in the court yard.

"So how's life been?" Jake asked and I could tell he was smiling because he sounded like he usually does when he plays around with me. I smiled and shook my head.

"You know the same old, same old" I said laughing when he let me take a bite out of my burger then taking a drink of my milk. I heard another person sit down.

"Hey Eve"

"Hi Sam, how were your classes?" I asked my sister while Jake put a fry in my mouth. We all talked until it was time for us to go back to class. I accidentally bumped into someone while we were walking. The guy yelled at me and I could feel how mad Jake was by his tense muscles. I turned my head to where I heard the guy yell.

"I'm sorry! I didn't mean to!" I yelled at him but didn't get a response I was about to yell again when Jake just started walking with me again. I turned my head back to look up and try to met Jakes eyes.

"But-" "Evangeline don't try. He didn't look back, that was Edrick Evans he doesn't like anyone except his friends and family" Jake said I nodded my head which my eyebrows scrunched together walking to wherever Jake walked me to. We made it to our class and Jake saw how distressed I was about the situation that just happened and he wrapped an arm around me pecking my lips telling me how it would be ok. I believe him and went to listening to our teacher.   ****I
hope you all like the first update! Love you my magical sea unicorns! Next chapter will be Edrick's.

How was the first update?

Did you all like it?

Chapter 2- Humans

Edrick's Pov"Edrick get your fat butt off of me!" Zoey my little sister yelled at me I laughed and put my full weight on her and she groaned. We were in her room she was laying down before I came in and tackled her off of her bed.

"Mom! Dad!" She yelled and I knew I was going to get in trouble for this. I got up off of her and threw myself of the bed picking up the book she was reading and pretend I was reading it and both my parents came in with their arms crossed together standing together looking intimidating.

"Edrick what were you doing to your poor sister?" Mom asked tapping her foot looking at me. Dad looked like he was about to use his Alpha voice and I really didn't want that cause it's just really weird cause he's my dad.

"I wasn't doing anything I swear I was just reading your book on her bed until she came in here yelling at me and she tried to tackle me so I moved out of her way and she landed on the floor and she threw a hissy fit!" I said putting the book down standing over my mother and sister. Me and dad were about the same height at 6'5 while mom was at 5'9 and Zoey was at 5'6.

"Edrick. What did you do?" Dad said gruffly using a little of his Alpha voice I flinched a little and put my head down and submitted to him.

"I came in here and tackled her off the bed.." I mumbled and he sighed pitching the bridge of his nose while mom shook her head and Zoey just chuckled at their reactions. I growled at her and she growled back until we were on the floor wrestling.

"Stop this right now!" Dad yelled using his full Alpha voice which made us both flinch and whimper getting up from the floor. Mom calmed him down by rubbing his arm and he gathered her in his arms sticking his head in the crook of her neck, being mates and all it would help calm him down. I can't wait to find my mate. He ordered us to go get ready and go to school and we did exactly that. We both got into my truck and headed off to school.

"Why did dad go off so badly mom had to help him?" Zoey asked and I sighed I know why but I don't want Zoey to worry about it. So I shrugged and heard her sigh before looking and, out the window.

Why don't you tell her? My wolf Caden asked I sighed and closed my eyes for a second before opening them and looking back at the road. Because it would worry her, and she wouldn't be able to focus. I barely can especially close to my ceremony and birthday which means I'm going to find my mate. I said pulling into the schools parking lot. That makes sense, and you mean OUR mate. He said as I rolled my eyes and blocked him out so I could focus durning my classes. I walked in to get accompanied by my friends Max, Devon, and Xan while my sister went to hang out with her friends.

"So, your sisters looking good today" Devon said smirking looking at her butt while she walked away with her friends I growled at Devon making him show me his neck in submission. I smiled when he did and we walked off heading to our first class. Which I ignored the whole period. Soon it was lunch, I picked my food and sat out in the courtyard with my friends.

"Have you seen that one girl?" I heard Devon mumble to Xan. I raised my head towards Devon and arched an eyebrow at him.

"This girl has been at our school forever and she is a human along with Jake and her sister, they're the only humans in this school. But I heard they moved around a lot! And she's not once looked anyone in the eye except teachers, Jake, and her sister Sam" Max said looking over at her smile her back facing us while she spoke with her sister and the boy.

"Ok? And? Does it really matter?" I grumble while sticking a fry into my mouth. Devon and Max raised their hands in defense.

"Their just saying cause we helped her once cause she bumped into us once and she asked if we could take her to Jake we did and he looked quite upset with her and we only picked up a little of their conversation cause we were a long ways from them. Jake said he was upset for trying to walk by herself, but we didn't fully understand it" Xan said I shrugged not caring for the blonde. Soon their class was called and the boy got her plate along with his and dumped it walking to her again helping her up leading her out. Interesting.

"See, it's odd that he always helps her around" Max said taking a drink from her water. I watched them walk back into the school disappearing from sight I could still smell their human scents though one was odd though. I looked back at my friends who sniffed the air until they picked up a scent they didn't want to smell blind shook their heads crinkling their noses. I laughed at them and they huffed.

"Dude why do it at school? Why not somewhere else like a bedroom? Bathroom? Dang it! Even the floor! But at school? They know we can smell that!" Xan complained we all laughed at him and got up dumping our trays heading back to class. While I was heading back I bumped into someone I didn't mind looking at them I just told them to watch where they were going, because everyone here is a werewolf except the girl, Jake, and her sister and I doubt I bumped into one of them. And while I was walking off I heard a petite voice yell sorry. I ignored it and growled walking to my class. Stupid humans. ****I hope you guys like Edrick's Pov! Until next time my magical sea unicorns!

So Evangeline goes to a all werewolf school?

Does Jake know about this?

When will they figure out she's blind?

Chapter 3- Realistic Dream

Evangeline's PovDreamI could see... I saw everything I see these weird things that have things sprouting from them I think those... Are trees.. I walked around through the many trees and found a opening with things sticking up from the ground.. Grass. I stood in the middle looking around until a huge thing came up and walked forwards.

I coward away from of how big it was and because I could feel the intense power radiating off of it. I could already tell you this was an animal but what was in? It looks like it would be similar to what a dog looks like maybe? Jake told me a wolf its something similar to a dog.

"Please.. Please don't hurt me.." I said to the wolf as I fell back and the massive black wolf kept walking towards me its amber eyes staring at me intently. I scrapped my arm and squealed at the pain I closed my eyes hearing the wolf growl. I braced myself for the pain but it never came. I felt a rough wet thing lick my injury and when I opened my eyes the wolf was licking me. I slowly patted its huge head and it immediately snuggled into me and I feel asleep.___________End of dream

I woke up in my bed stretching my limbs out I kept my eyes close and then opened them meeting darkness. I wish that I just had one morning I woke up to colors and objects , I wonder if the things I saw in my dream actually looked like that..

I sighed dismissing my wish and thoughts while throwing my legs over my bed. I tried to be quite trying to do it by myself but I just ended up running into a wall falling back onto my butt. I groaned as I heard my bedroom door open and I swung my head to look in the direction of the noise and I heard someone sigh.

"Are you anxious to go to school?" Jake asked me I sighed as he lead me to my closet. Jake lives with us because his parents gave him up when he was 8 or 9 and my family and I have known him since I was just a baby.

"No.. I just wanted to try and do something by myself. I mean I could probably eat and put my own clothes on if I tried!" I complained while I sat in a chair while he looked through my closet deciding what I should wear. I heard him grunt and walk over to me.

"So, what did ya pick out today" I said sighing because I know he wouldn't answer we back.

"Your wearing camouflage t-shirt, washed out shorts, and white tennis shoes. And if you want to try to put your own clothes on go ahead and try" he said laying a pile of clothes beside me. I squealed and got up and picked out whatever was on top I felt it and thunk but Jake told me it was my shirt and I grumbled. I slid my head into the shirt and then my arms and put my pants on and then my shoes.

"Ta da!" I shouted raising my hands up smiling looking forward hoping I was looking straight as him. He sighed before taking off my shirt putting it on telling me it was on backwards. Then took my shoes off and switched them.

"Other than those mistakes you did good" he said and I smiled a little glad that I did ok. We went downstairs to eat and I walked on Jakes arm confidently and sat down and heard a clink it front of me and I smiled looking straight hoping Jake will let me try.

"Fine" he said sitting beside me, my smile grew wider as I patted the table to feel for a fork when I felt it I picked it up and started trying to find my plate. Jake moved my hand over and I felt something soft. I stabbed it and picked it up and put it all in my mouth. It was a pancake so I bit into it making the rest fall onto the plate.. I think it was the plate.

"Evangeline you drop your pancake on the floor" Jake sighed, I sighed and told him he could feed me. He did and mom, dad, and Lily told us goodbye, Lily just barked while me, Jake, and Sam headed out and went to school. Me and Jake walked in while Sam walked to her class and so did me and Jake.

When we walked in Jake was greeted by one of his friends and while they were talking I just stood by him and fiddled with my fingers. I sighed and I think Jake heard me cause he told his friend he needed to head to class and we walked away.

"Hey? You ok?" Jake asked and I nodded my head, should I tell Jake about my dream? It was so realistic... I really am curious if that's what tress, grass, and wolves looked like. I shook my head silently to myself while we walked to our classroom. I felt like something weird is going to happen. I ignored it listening to class telling Jake my answers to our quiz. Once class was over our teacher told us to set the papers on his desk. We walked over there and our teacher stopped us before we left.

"Thank you guy for being my favorite in my class" he said and we both laughed and said you're welcome walking out. We were walking to our next class when someone came up and stopped us and it was Sam. She was whispering something really quite to Jake and I didn't catch it but I heard him mumbled an ok and he soon kept walked my while I yelled goodbye to Sam and she did the same. That was very very odd.... ****Hey may magical sea unicorns I'm actually keeping up with this book but this may be the last update in a while on both this book and my other one I have a lot on my plate right now and my friends our having problems I need to help with, I hope you all understand! Thank you!

Why did Evangeline have that weird dream?

What is going to happen?

Why did Sam stop Jake in the hall?

Chapter 4- Ceremony

E drick's PovI didn't go to school today because it's my birthday today and mom and dad said they needed me here for the ceremony. So I've been here helping everyone get everything ready. I watched as my sister played with the omegas and runts. We weren't one those kind of packs who treated omegas and runts differently we all are equally.

Mostly because my sister is an runt she has Alpha blood in her but the runt gene was stronger; my mom is an omega and my dad is an Alpha, I am full Alpha, I don't have any omega or runt genes but I'm a hybrid. My mom is a vampire and my dad is an Alpha he is the king of all werewolves and vampires but his main concern is always on our pack. The only omega trait I have is goofing around but only with my family.

"Edrick the ceremony is close, you better start getting ready" Zoey said walking in with her purple silky dress. I smiled at her and she looked down at herself and then at me.

"Do I look ok?" She asked and I smiled and nodded, me and Zoey are twins I call her my little sister though cause I was born before her. She wants to look good because she wants to look good for her mate if she finds him tonight. I got up with a sigh and went into my closet picking out my suit and dress shoes. After I got my suit on I walked out of my room downstairs where my family was waiting for me.

"Oh honey. I'm so happy!" Mom cried hugging me I hugged her back smiling. I pulled back and saw my dad walk in with a huge amount of power radiating off of him. I've always looked up to him, I've always followed his rules and wishes to be here right now having my ceremony getting ready to take the Alpha position. He smiled at me opening his arms and I walked to him hugging him. Zoey awed and I snorted at her and she chuckled.

"Let's go it's close to 12 and this party isn't going to stop till 4 AM" Zoey said shaking her hips. We all laughed at her while we walked out. Dad went up there getting everyone's attention and did his speech before calling me up.

"Repeat after me" dad said making a cut into the palm of my hand and his holding them together over a bowl. "Do you Edrick Jace Evans, accept the role as Alpha of The Blue Moon Pack, and the packs and clans around the nation" he said and I repeated after him taking the weight off his shoulders.

"I, Edrick Jace Evans accept the role as Alpha of The Blue Moon Pack, and the packs and clans around the nation" I said confidently feeling all the weight of my pack and everything else. I winched a little bit it eased and took my hand away letting my hand heal. Dad patted my back smiling and welcomed me as my pack cheered. Mom and Zoey came up and stood with us as we counted down the clock till midnight. And as soon as it it I was 18 and I was ready to find my mate. All eligible women and men were in the front and me and Zoey sniffed. I smelled nothing but cheap perfume and their scents. I was sad but I saw Zoey's eyes darken as she looked around all the men perked up but she looked over beside her and Mason was there our betas son which is our new beta of the pack.

"Mine" he growled as he pulled her into his arms Zoey sighed in content and I smiled as we congratulated her. Mom and dad looked at me and I just shook my head and they sighed dismissing everyone to go have fun and party all the women and men huffed upset and went off I got off the stage and went to Zoey and Mason. Mason doesn't go to school cause he works more on his beta duties.

"Hey Zoey, congratulations on finding your mate" I said and she smiled while blushing at Masons arm wrapped around her.

"Thanks, did you not find your mate?" She asked and I nodded giving her a small smile trying to seem ok. She frowned at me and came to me hugging me.

"I'm sorry bub, maybe she's at school, you know there's other packs close to us" she said and I nodded and we pulled away walking with her mate into the crowd. I sighed while I stood next to my parents shaking everyone's hands cause I didn't know what else to do cause I don't have my mate yet and I was planing on finding her tonight and getting to know her.

"Honey, why don't you go and party with the rest of the pack?" I shrugged looking at everyone, it didn't look as fun as it would be. I sighed and told her I would go for a run, she nodded and let me go I ran into the forest and hid behind a tree taking my clothes off and shifting into my big black wolf.

Well that was disappointing.. Caden said while running around in the woods taking control running off to his favorite place no one knows about except us. Our secret cave that's hidden from the world by vines and grass with a pond and waterfall in it. I know, I was hoping we would find our mate.. I said as he walked into the cave laying next to the pond watching the waterfall hit the water peacefully while we listened to all the creatures and sounds of the forest. We will find our mate, and that's a promise. He said before blocking me out letting me have control. I closed my eyes relaxing beside the pond.

We will find you my little mate. And I promise when I find you, I won't let you go. No matter what.. ****So I hope you all liked this chapter from now on the chapters will stay focused on Evangeline's Pov. I love you all!

What will Edrick do when he goes to school and finds his mate?

How will Evangeline react?

How will Edrick react when he figures out who his mate is?

Chapter 5- Mad Stranger

Evangeline's PovMe and Jake where already at school in our first period while Jake took down notes for us while I listened trying to memorize as much as I can. After we were done we got up and walked out walking to our next class. Today Jake dressed me in shots, tank top, a cardigan, and my converse, with my hair braided. He also put the necklace he got for me in it was a ying yang symbol. My classes went by and it was lunch time but I had a huge test so I got my lunch and took it to the library with Jake. We studied until the bell rung.

"Well we ate a nutritious lunch and studied, we're going to ace this test!" Jake said to me and I laughed cause I could tell he had a goofy smile on his face I smiled at him and he kissed me and we went into our class getting ready for our test. Me and Jake are the sweet soft couple but I remember once we had a really hot make out session. And just thinking about it makes me blush.

"What are you blushing about?" Jake whispered to me I shivered and blushed harder and he stopped and turned me around where I was facing him. I could feel him intensely watching me.

"Just thinking..."

"About?.."

"Our make out session" I said really quietly and Jake chuckled hugging me pulling me close to his body by my waist while my hands were on his chest. I felt his breathe on my neck making me shiver. He planted soft kisses on my neck and I smiled softly but frowned when he stopped I opened my eyes meeting darkness giving him a pouty face.

"Not here little one" he said and we walked out to our class. I sighed and let him take me to old boring class. When we got in we jumped right into notes and while I told him what to write down I felt his hand on my thigh. I smiled speaking and pushed it away I heard him grumble and put it back. He stayed like that the whole class and soon the class was over and the rest of the day flew by. We were walking out of school while his arm was wrapped around my waist guiding me. Then all you heard was a huge powerful snarl. I flinched and we suddenly stopped and Jake turned around with us. I heard someone walk towards us and I tensed and I felt Jake tense.

"Mine" the guy in front is lowly growled. His voice made me melt inside, but yet I gripped Jakes arm because I was kinda scared. Did we have something we have? I don't think so. I kept my head down not showing him my eyes. He jerked me out of Jakes hold which made me freak out and struggle against his grip. How can people not see this? I could hear Jake struggle to get free from something, I put my head in the direction of the noise and my eyebrows scrunched together. Until something gripped my chin making me look up. I close my eye getting accompanied by darkness like usual.

"Open those pretty eyes of yours Vasílissa mou" he said I shook my head and he growled holding me closer to his body. I let a tear fall from my cheek while I sniffed hearing Jake struggle.

"Get away from her! I'll kill you if you even think about hurting a hair on her head!" Jake yelled and the stranger holding me growled loudly holding me closer to him.

"She's mine! You can't tell me what to do with her!" The man roared I let a sob out while my eyes were still closed and the stranger pulled back looking at my tears. I felt a warm hand on my cheek.

"Please don't cry Vasílissa mou" he said I pushed at his chest and stumbled back onto the ground scrapping my elbow I yelled out in pain opening my eyes. I heard a gasp and someone help me up but it didn't feel warm and tingly.

"It's ok little one. I'm here" Jake said I grabbed onto his arm and gasped having a panic attack looking around frantically even though I couldn't see anything.

"I'm so sorry Vasílissa mou" the guy said and I gasped breathing hard.

"Dude... She's blind" someone said I put my head in that direction and closed my eyes looking down trying to catch my breath. Jake picked me up and walked away with me. I heard a growl that scared me even more. I started shaking in Jakes arms but he shushed me but for some reason I didn't calm down and usually I would. He sat me in a seat and closed a door. Then I heard another door open and close. Then a sound of a car starting which told me we were in the car going home.

"Are you ok?" Jake asked and I nodded catching my breath. I just want to curl up in bed. Wait.. We forgot Sam.. Great

Edrick's PovMy mate is blind... She's blind. And she's a human. I stood in the parking lot thinking about when her eyes first opened they were a beautiful white color but I realized she was blind and she's human and she has a boyfriend! She's mine and I will take her away from him. Even though she's blind and human I still want her. And I WILL have her.

Our mate is beautiful. Caden said and I nodded

She's beautiful and we will kill that human. Axel my vampire said and I sighed. It's nice to hear from you Axel. I said and he nodded while they both stayed silent. Max, Devon, and Xan were standing amazed of who their Luna is.

"She's blind" Max said quietly and I nodded walking towards them, she looked so scared of me.. She had to have felt the tingles of the mate bond. I growled just thinking about how that human had his hands all over her. Caden was riled up about it. I couldn't take this much stress. I shifted into my black wolf ripping my clothes and ran into the woods. ****Sorry I love Edrick's Pov lol. Love you all my magical sea unicorns!

What did you all think of that?

Edrick still wants her

Will Evangeline accept Edrick or reject him?

Chapter 6- New Escort

E vangeline's Pov I woke up in my bed with tears on my cheeks and I could already tell you my eyes were puffy from crying. The only reason I did cry is because when I have a panic attack they are really bad.

"Are you ok?" Jake asked from behind me, I made him stay with me last night. I nodded and sat up I heard him sit up too wrapping his arms around me making me sit in his lap where I straddled him, I wrapped my arms around his neck and dug my head into his neck while he did the same.

"It'll be ok. Today will be just fine, I promise I won't let him come near you" Jake said talking about the guy from yesterday. I replied with a small ok and got up while he led me to my closet picking out clothes. He told me I was wearing a white dress, black flats, my hair curled with a black bow, and my necklace Jake gave me. We walked out and I heard small barks and I smiled crouching down and let Lily come to me licking me while I giggled.

"Come on little one. We have to go to school. Sam! Come one! We're leaving!" Jake yelled helping me up and guiding me out. She yelled back and we all headed to school. When we walked in Jakes arm was around me like usual and then all you heard was a huge ferocious snarl. I looked around even if I couldn't see anything while my breathe picked up. Jake whispered it was ok into my ear while he guided me to our classroom. Once we got in there he told me he had to get his and my paper from our Rachel's desk because he wasn't here yet and he wanted us to get a head start. I heard a loud thud and someone speak but I ignored it while looking down.

"Hello Vasílissa mou, it seems like your friend Jake had to go home for an emergency. So I will be helping you today" someone said and I recognized the voice from yesterday it was that guys voice the one who stopped me and Jake in the parking lot. I still looked down not wanted to look up and show him my eyes. I heard him pull a chair beside me and set papers on the desk.

"giatí mou édoses énan tóso athóo sýntrofo? allá sas efcharistó theá tis selínis mou" the guy said wrapping his arm around me. For some reason I didn't feel threatened or anything except comfort and small tingles on my skin. I melted into his arms sighing making him growl in satisfaction. Class begun and I heard our teacher walk in and gasp as did everyone else. I opened my eyes from where they were shut and looked in around confused.

"I would suggest that you all turned around and minded your own business before I get mad" the guy holding me said and I heard chairs scoot against the floor while everything else was silent.

"So Vasílissa mou, what's your name?"

"Erm.. It's Evangeline... Evangeline Meadows Rose" I said giving him my full name, I don't know who this person is and I don't know where Jake went and if it was the real reason but yet I have this stranger my full name. He sighed and kissed the side of my head. I have a small smile but remember Jake, I have a boyfriend that I love dearly I can't just do this.

"So, what's your name?" I asked scooting away from him and I heard him growl and pull me back while I felt his warm breath on my neck making me shiver in delight.

"My name is Edrick Jace Evans" he said kissing the curve of my neck making tingles shoot up and down my body.

"Erm. E-Edrick I don't know if you know t-this or not but I have a boyfrie-nd. I'm not implying anyth-ing! But I'm just saying that J-Jake wouldn't like me doing this. I m-mean I'm not a cheater and I woul-dn't do that do h-him. But I'm also not s-saying your doing anything-g wrong! You're just being f-friendly" I said blabbing about Jake and what not. I heard Edrick huff and then chuckle at me which the sudden movement of his chest against my arm shot tingles up and down my arm making me shiver.

"It'll be ok Vasílissa mou, he won't mind. I'm just helping you out for today" he said and I nodded and told him to write down notes for me I felt a sudden movement telling me he nodded and wanted me to tell me what he wanted me to write down. We went the day like this him growling at things and helping me out and soon it was lunch and I got to see my sister Sam. We sat down at a table and Edrick started feeding me.

"Erm. Hey Eve, who's this?" Sam asked sitting next to me and I smiled cause after the few periods me and Edrick had together we have became good friends and I wanted to introduce Sam to him.

"Sam this is Edrick my friend, and Edrick this is my sister Sam. Jake had to go home so Edrick is helping me today" I said and she hummed while we sat, ate, and talked until the bell rung. Soon all my other classes zoomed by and it was time to go home. Edrick was nice enough to give me and Sam a ride home. When we walked through the door I was tackled into a hug.

"Evangeline!" Jakes voice said making me smile and laugh at him hugging him back. But oddly I didn't feel pleasant tingles when I hugged Jake, but I did when I hugged Edrick.

"I'm so happy you're home" he said pulling back but resting his head on mine. I frowned and pulled back more looking at where his voice came from and scrunched my eyebrows together.

"What? Why? Is everything ok?" I asked and he pulled me back into him hugging the life out of me.

"Yea I'm just glad you're home" he said and I nodded unsure and we went into the kitchen meeting my loving family. ****I'm really tired my magical sea unicorns so no questions or cute little messages today. Hope you liked the chapter!

Chapter 7- New Friends and Proposals

Evangeline's Pov"Hey, Evangeline. Wake up. It's homecoming week. Today is the day you get to show off your dress and tomorrow is country club vs country attire"Jake said and I nodded getting up and stretching. I wonder if Jake is going to ask me to homecoming.. It's on Friday and today is Monday.. Hm.. I got up and let Jake help me into my homecoming dress, makeup, my hair done, and my heels. He then went behind me and put on my ying yang necklace.

"You look beautiful" Jake said and I blushed while smiling and said thank you. He lead me down stairs and my parents cried looking at us.

"You all look so beautiful in your dresses! And you look very handsome Jake" mom said and I heard Jake laugh beside of me, I shook my head smiling to myself and I heard a camera going off.

"Let's go guys. We need to get to school" Sam said while laughing a little, we headed out and got into Jakes car and we headed to school. When we made it Jake told me to stay put so he could open the door for me. I waited till I heard him open my door I reached my hand out for him and he took it helping me out. He pulled me into him pecking my lips when he pulled away I was smiling but then I heard a loud snarl. I looked around trying to find where the noise came from. I heard Jake take a breathe in and start walking with me.

"Jake? Are you ok?" I asked and I felt him peck my forehead and mumble a small yes. I hummed in response wondering what was wrong with him. I shrugged it off and we both walked to our class. Jake told me everyone looked nice in their homecoming attire. I imagined everyone in there suits and their homecoming dresses and what they looked like.

"Ready for lunch" Jake asked and I nodded and we headed to our usual table until Jake stopped me and sat me down somewhere else.

"Hello Vasílissa mou, you look beautiful" I heard Edrick say I smiled and thanked him.

"Jake this is my new friend! His other friends should be her soon" I said thinking I heard a low growl but I dismissed it and went back to eating the food Jake fed me. I would hear a growl every now and then but I ignored it.

"Hey Eve, hey Jake, hey.. Edrick?" I heard Sam say sitting down next to me. I turned to her and smiled. I tried to start a conversation but everyone was just awkward and Sam would only talk to me and Jake, Jake would only talk to me or Sam, and Edrick only talked to me until his friends got here but he still talked to me the most. After lunch was over I felt Jake guide me back to class but then I heard Edrick.

"Hey, I will take her back to class" he said but it didn't sound like a asking tone is sounded like he was demanding for him to give me up. Soon I was pulled into warmth and sparked igniting over my waist and arms.

"Let's go to class Vasílissa mou" he said and a shiver went down my spine as we walked to our next class. We soon made it and I sat down but was soon pulled onto a lap and nuzzled into a hard chest but was oddly comfortable to me. I sighed and snuggled deeper into the warmth allowing my whole body to spread tingles.

"Your so cute" I heard Edrick say while the teacher talked.

"Edrick you should start writing down notes for me. Please" I said and he sighed and adjusted me and started writing down notes that I told him too. Soon all my classes were over and it was time for everyone to go home. Me and Edrick we're walking out when a snarl was beside me. It wasn't the small low ones I've heard before it was a huge dominating one, I coward back but was pulled back into a warm chest.

"Hey dude let her go!"

"You're going to get in trouble by your father!"

"Alpha won't like this.."

What are they talking about? Alpha? What? Soon the warmth was off of me and I heard Jake in front of me.

"Star light star bright. 1st star I see tonight. I wish you may. I wish you might. Be my date on homecoming night" Jake said and I cried silently cause I knew he got a poster and write it on it. I nodded my head and felt arms wrap around me but I didn't feel the tingles and warmth like when Edrick hugged me... What am I thinking.. I have a boyfriend that I love dearly.

"I love you"

"I love you too Jake" then i kisses him and when we pulled apart I heard an awful roar, I wrapped my arms around Jake but then everything was silent from then.

"It's ok little one. Let's go home" he said I nodded and we got into his car while Sam was squealing over the fact Jake asked me to homecoming. I laughed at her and soon we were home and the same happened with my mom. Dad just threatened Jake like any other normal dad but they ended up laughing at each other, Lilly was yapping and I could hear her paws running around like a wild child.

"Honey, you know I'm so proud of you" mom said and I could tell by her voice she was crying from happiness. I smiled and nodded while I pulled her into a hug. She clung on to me as I did her.

"I love you mama" I said and she sniffled and pulled back grabbing my face stroking it.

"I love you too baby girl" dad and Sam soon joined. And we had a big group hug then Jake and Lily joined. I love them all so much. ***Hey guys.... Please don't kill me. I'm sorry I haven't been alive in like.. 300 weeks. But band has kept me busy! Hope you all like the update!

What did Evangeline hear?

Will Edrick stop them from going to homecoming?

What will happen next?

Chapter 8- Rouges

E drick's PovDevon, Xan, and Max took me to the woods to shift. They
watched me claw at trees and tear things up. I growled with so much
power they all bowed there heads.

Shift I said through our mind link, Devon's Wolf was black, Max's Wolf
was blonde, and Xan's was brown. We all ran to the pack house and went
inside shifting back putting on clothes. How dare that human ask our mate
to homecoming! Axel yelled and Caden growled loudly in agreement. I
shut them out but nodded to them before I did.

Alpha! Marcus yelled through the mind link. What is it Marcus? Having
mate problems with my sister? I asked smirking I heard him huff before
beginning to talk again. No! Rogues are attacking the south borders and
more are coming through the north, west, and east borders! There all
attacking at once! Once he was done I gave him instructions to get all the
omegas, runts, women, children, and elderly in the safe house, and to get
all the warriors to each border I stood my ground close to the safe house
protecting everyone. Then I smelt it, strawberry's and fresh water. I looked
around and saw Evangeline in the middle of everything looking around in
terror trying to find the noise. I growled and looked at my people and then
at her and shook my head closing my eyes.

Save mate! Caden yelled at me and I shook my head again clenching my eyes. Save her now! Axel yelled louder and I growled loudly making everyone stop and look at me and Evangeline looked toward me with crunched up eyebrows with tears down her face. Then a wolf tackled her down making her scream. And that was it I charged toward them seeing that Marcus took over my position. I tackled the wolf off of her and snapped at his face realizing it was one of my warriors.

What do you think your doing?! I yelled at him through the mind link. He whimpered and submitted to me. I'm sorry Alpha I didn't know she was yours. He whimpered and I let him go. It doesn't matter we don't attack innocent humans! Especially women! Now go back to fighting! I yelled he ran off while I looked at Evangeline. I nuzzled my snout on her cheek and she hugged onto my neck and I put her on my back running off back to the safe house. I pushed her in it and told them to keep her safe that she was their Luna. Then I went back to fighting.

Evangeline's Pov I just wanted to talk a simple walk but instead got lost in the woods in the middle of wolves fighting. I got pushed somewhere by a wolf that was very nice to me saved me.

"Luna? Hello Luna. Are you ok?" A women asked I didn't know who Luna was but I wanted help and security so I looked around looked for a hand I felt one and she pulled me into her chest letting me sob.

"Oh. She's blind" I heard someone say and whispers started cascading through the whole room. Then I felt a wrinkly hand on my forehead and cheek. I looked up and felt the person gasped.

"To dikó sas. Esý eísai to paidí pou tha mas sósei ólous. To paidí tis theás tou fengarioú" the old women said and everyone gasped. I scrunched my eyebrows together and tilted my head and heard a crash and everyone scream but then it was silent. Literally everything was silent. Then the door creaked open and everyone gasped.

"Alpha. Are you ok?" Someone asked and then there was a whimper/growl and then a thud. Everyone started freaking out and they started yelling for help and I heard growls and whimpers. I started freaking out until the familiar wrinkly hand touched me again.

"It's ok child. Go to sleep" she said running her fingers over my forehead and oddly my eyes started to feel heavy and I fell into a deep sleep.

DreamI woke up in a black space with water on the ground. And the odd part was. I could see. I walked around trying to look for something or anyone.

"Hello? Is anyone here?" I yelled and it just echoed. I walked around even more until I saw a silhouette of something. I ran towards it seeing a tall muscular man.

"Vasílissa mou..." the guy said hugging me to him making tingles form everywhere and I realized it was Edrick. I pulled back and looked at his face and felt his face with my hands.

"Is this really what you look like Edrick?" I asked and he laughed gentle pulling my hands from his face to his mouth pecking them slightly making tingles explode everywhere while I gasped from them. He smiled and looked from my hands taking them to his chest resting them there while he pulled me closer to him by my waist.

"Yes, it is. Do you want to see yourself?" He asked and I nodded and he turned me around in his arms and I saw myself. My eyes were a beautiful color my long hair was vibrant and lively then my skin was so clear.

"You look beautiful Vasílissa mou" he said turning me to him and slowly pulling me in. Our breathes were colliding from how close we were and when he pulled me the to his lips everything faded.

"Edrick?" I asked and heard a whimper. I looked around seeing a silhouette of something on the ground. I walked closer and the more I got closer the more whimpering and pained howls I heard. When I was finally there there was a beautiful golden wolf laying on the floor with silver chains around in and a silver chain on its muzzle making it whimper and bleed. She looked at me and something clicked.

"Wake up Evangeline. Wake up now! Get out of here!" The wolf yelled in a beautiful angelic voice I looked at it walking back away from it and seeing a huge shadow cascade down on us making me scream and put my hands over my head for protection.___________End of dream

I woke up gasping looking around seeing darkness again. Where am I? ***Hope you all like the update! :)

What did the Rouges want?

What happened to Edrick? Is he ok?

Who was that silver wolf?

Chapter 9- Werewolves

E vangeline's PovI listened trying to hear something until a heard feet walking toward my room so I snuggled back into the blankets and pretended I was asleep. Someone walked into my room and I clenched my eyes closed and waited for them to leave.

"I know you're awake" the voice said and I sighed and rolled over keeping my eyes closed knowing all to well that I won't see anything.

"Open your eyes for me Vasílissa mou" I sighed again and opened my eyes meeting darkness. I scrunched my eyebrows and closed my eyes again embarrassed to show a stranger my eyes.

"Your eyes are beautiful, please show me them" he whispered into my ear making me shiver. I opened my eyes looking at the darkness that consumed me. I felt a warm hand on my cheek and I instantly knew it was Edrick.

"Edrick? Where am I? What is going on? Wha-"

"Sh Vasílissa mou, your at my house and I will tell you what's going on later. Right now you need to eat" he said and I nodded and sat up allowing him to help me out if the bed with a tiny groan. I looked towards him and tilted my head.

"Are you ok? Are you hurt?" I asked him and he sighed sitting me back onto the bed and I felt a dip beside me letting me know he sat on the bed beside of me.

"I got injured yesterday but I'm ok" he said and I looked down and sat up reaching out for his hand. He took mine and I pulled him up and pulled him towards the direction I believed the door was at.

"What are you doing?"

"I'm going to help you, you can give me directions and I'll take them" I said and he sighed and pulled away from me. I whined and reached my hands out and tried to feel for him but he took my hands and held them.

"You are not doing such a thing, I'm fine I can handle taking you downstairs" he said and I mumbled under my breath while he showed me the way and groaning every now and then. Once we made it downstairs into the kitchen he sat me down and I heard him stumble and whimper. And when I say whimper I don't mean like a human whimper I mean an animalistic whimper. I gasped and he covered it up with a couch and a question.

"What would you like to eat?" He asked and I thought for a second before answering with toast with jelly on it. He mumbled a small ok and I heard him shuffling through cabinets. Then someone else walked in and started talking to Edrick and completely ignoring me.

"Hey Edrick! Mom and dad told me to tell you that there is a meeting in the yard today to warn the pack about the rou-"

"Zoey, calm down. I know. And don't talk about that stuff in front of Evangeline. I haven't told her about all that yet" Edrick said and I looked in the direction of his voice tilting my head. What pack? What does she mean? Then I heard a loud squeal making me cower back. I've always had good hearing.

"Hello! I'm Edrick's sister! Zoey! It's nice to meet you Evangeline! I thought Edrick would be a lonely grouch forever!" She yelled and hugged me making me blush. Edrick laughed and sat a plate in front of me then handed me a piece of my toast letting me eat it myself. I smiled and thanked him.

"Now Zoey go so I may talk to her" he said and she huffed leaving while yelling bye. I laughed and waved and heard Edrick sigh.

"Now your probably wondering what's going on. God it's too early to be telling you." He said mum the last sentence. I nodded and he sighed sitting next to me.

"So. I'm going to try to explain this in the most easiest and gentlest way I can. So um, do you believe in magical beings? Like werewolves, vampires, etc?" He asked and I shrugged I never asked myself if werewolves and stuff like that were real.

"Well. I am one of those magical creatures. The fight you walked into yesterday was my pack and rouges fighting. Rouges are werewolves that don't have a pack most are bad and evil that try to take down packs and take innocent human lives away. But we don't kill rouges unless they need to be killed. Packs are a group of werewolves ruled by an Alpha and Luna and I am the Alpha. I am not a regular werewolf though. I'm a hybrid. Of a werewolf and vampire" he said and I was taken back. I gasped, I wasn't scared of Edrick but I was shocked by all this information and oddly I believe him.

"Werewolves have mates. The Moon Goddess which is the Goddess who created us, gives us our other halves that were perfectly made for us to be with forever and to cherish and love, we can't live without them. And Evangeline you are my mate. You are going to be the Luna of this pack" he said and I shook my head. I have a boyfriend, that I love dearly. I can't do this to him. It isn't right.

"Edrick I'm honored, but I can't. I have a boyfriend. I can't just break up with him because I'm your mate." I said and I heard a growl. And by the dominance it radiated I assumed it was Edrick.

"Evangeline you are mine, that mutt can not take you away from me. Do you not feel anything when I touch you? Can you not feel the connection we have?" He said pulling me to him so I was straddling his waist making me blush. I felt sparks everywhere making me subconsciously lean against him.

"Please Vasílissa mou. Please don't reject me. I love you already" ***I hope you guys like the update and I'm sorry if it's moving too fast! Tell me if I am so I can slow down! Love you all my magical sea unicorns!

What will Evangeline do?

Who will she choose?

What will Edrick do if she chooses Jake?

Chapter 10- Meeting the Parents

Edrick's PovIt's the day after I told Evangeline everything and she had to go with me to a pack meeting. Everyone kept huddling over her making me have to use my Alpha voice to get them to all step back. Today is school and I don't have any girl clothes. Zoey said she could borrow some of her clothes and I thanked her. I told Zoey to only give me pants and shoes for her and she can wear one of my hoodies. I let her change herself and she walked out with the wrong shoes on her feet. I laughed and helped her with her tiny mistakes. She blushed when I was done and smiled at me.

"Thank you Edrick" she said and I smiled liking the way my name sounded from her. Caden and Axel growled in pleasure making me growl lowly enough so she didn't hear me. I picked her up off the bed and held her hand guiding her down stairs where my mom and dad will probably be. They didn't get to see her yesterday and they don't know she is blind so I don't know how they will handle it.

"Edrick! Let me see your beautiful mate! Stop hogging her!" Mom yelled and pulled Evangeline out of my arms making me growl and mom shushed me.

"Hello! I'm Edrick's mom! It's so nice to meet you!" She said putting a hand out for Evangeline to shake. Evangeline stood there and smiled getting ready to say something but got cut off my dad.

"Honey she can't see your hand, she's blind. And she's a human" dad said coming from behind mom sniffing Evangeline making her uncomfortable. I came from behind Evangeline and pulled her to me making her relax.

"Yes she is all of those things but that doesn't change anything. I love her dearly and will do anything for her and she will be the Luna of this pack" I said and dad nodded firmly walking out. I sighed and my mom shook her head.

"Honey I'm sorry that happened. But you will be a fine Luna for this pack. And I assume Edrick here has already told you everything?" Mom said and Evangeline nodded smiling while mom held her hands. She made a happy noise and leaded her to the dinning table sitting her down and engaged her into a conversation while Zoey watched and joined in. I smiled and shook my head seeing them feed her. I looked at the clock and went to get Zoey and Evangeline.

"It's time to go. Bye mom I love you" I said and she said it back while we all head out. We made it to school and the human she always walked around with was looking everywhere. Jake. Ugh. He saw us and started running over to us. I gripped her hips tighter and then she was pulled out of my arms making me growl lowly.

"Evangeline! Your family and I have been worried sick about you! Where did you go?" He asked her and she sighed and tensely leaned into him making me growl again.

"I-I just wanted to go for a walk by myself in the woods and I went to far and got lost and then I bumped into Edrick and he helped me" she said and he nodded and looked over at me.

"Thank you for taking care of her" he said and I nodded to him and he walked off with Evangeline in his arms. I watched at they disappeared making me into a growling fit.

I'm going to rip the mutt piece to piece, Axel growled making Caden snarl and agreed with him, I simply growled back showing that I liked the idea making my eyes turn red from blood lust. Then I felt a hand on my shoulder making me spin around and go off on the person.

"What!" I yelled and I saw Max with Xan and Devon. She flinched back seeing my eyes red and my eyes turned normal, I sighed and rubbed my face.

"I'm sorry Max. I'm just a little on edge" I said and she looked at Devon and Xan and they patted my back.

"It's ok dude. You just need to get your blood lust under control. You're mom would hit you straight up the head if she saw you acting like this" Devon said and I smiled imagining my mom scolding me.

"Yea and your father would be upset seeing you so on edge and barley controlling your wolf and especially your vampire" Xan said acting as if vampires were the nastiest thing in the world, I growled at him showing my fangs and canines making him submit to me.

"Don't go lasts your limits Xan you may be my best friend but I have to maintain the peace between vampires and werewolves. Plus my mom and I are vampires you should respect us" I said and he whimpered and nodded. I nodded at them and we all headed to class. Soon it was lunch and I saw Evangeline, Jake, and Evangeline's sister, Sam. I mind linked Devon, Max, and Xan to sit there and they all nodded and sat.

"Hello Vasílissa mou" I said sitting down and she blushed and looked towards my voice not fully reaching my eyes.

"Hey Edrick" she whispered and I looked at Jake to see him giving a small glare and I rolled my eyes as he fed her.

"So. Thank you for helping my sister Edrick" Sam said and I nodded at her but something seemed off by Jake's and Sam's sent.. It smelt weird. I ignored it and went back eating and talking to Evangeline and my friends. Soon they had to go and it made Caden and Axel on edge when he lead her my the small of her waist.

"Careful Edrick" Max said and I nodded getting Caden and Axel under control making my eyes turn back into my original color. She will be the death of me.   ***I hope you liked the chapter you all! And thank you guys for being so sweet about my break up! I really appreciated it! Oh and if you all like science fiction you should all try my other book that I wrote with my best friend called Mystical and Mysterious! It is an old book we wrote so it is written differently.

What will Edrick do?

Is Evangeline growing feeling towards Edrick?

What will happen next?

Chapter 11- Training

Evangeline's PovI woke up in my bed and in my house. I sighed and swung my legs over the bed. My family is a traveling family. We move every few weeks to a new county. That's why I never got used to the walls and areas of a loving home. It's because I never had enough time to memorize the place. They've always treated me like a baby. I've never known what anything looks like so I don't know how to maneuver it. I sighed and got up try to feel my way around, I got confident in myself and went faster ending up bumping into a wall with me hands. I sighed and felt for a door handle and found one.

"Hopefully this is the closet" I said to myself and opened the door and tumbled into the room. I feel around and found another door handle it just lead to an amount of door handles until I found stairs. I know what I'm going to do. I made my way down stairs and felt around. I listened on the noises around me and opened the door I was hoping was the the back door. I stumbled outside and walked onto our porch and then I felt soft grass under my feet. I walked u til the ground got courser me realizing I was in the woods I put my hands out and felt around until I found an opening. I plopped down and start to scream.

"EDRICK! HELP ME! HELP!" I yelled and wailed until I felt a hush of air and someone pick me up.

"Evangeline? Are you ok!? What happened?! How did you make it out here?" He asked and I put my finger up stoping him from talking anymore.

"Edrick. Will you please train me? Help me to go on life without anyone helping me?" I asked and it was silent until I felt his hand on my cheek.

"Evangeline. What? Why? What do you mean?" He asked and I sighed letting myself lean into him.

"Everyone thinks I can't do anything by myself. They all think I'm stupid. I can't even walk through my own house and memorize everything because we move every few weeks!" I said legging tears fall from my eyes.

"Shh. It's ok. I will train you" he cooed and I jumped into his arms happily. I whispered a thank you to him and felt his chest vibrate while he purred. I smiled while he picked me up and carried me off.

"We will start today but first you need to change into some work out clothes. I can get us to be excused for school" he said and I nodded. Soon we were at his house and he went off somewhere to get me clothes. He came back and told me to change and lead me to a room. I grunted and started to feel the clothes. Hm. I put on the tank top he gave me and then the leggings and they all felt right so I walked out.

"Did I put them on right?" I asked and Edrick said yes and lead me outside. And that's where we started until close to the end of the day.

"Remember Evangeline listen to your surroundings. Feel the earth beneath your feet" he said and I tried my best. Edrick was walking and I tried to listen where he was. He finally stopped and I walked where I thought he was.

"Did I do it?" I asked and he grunted not giving me a clear answer. But the thing is I heard it not in front of me but to the right of me. I turned my head right and sighed.

"You were close but listen when you become Luna a rogue attack may happen. I need you to be able to keep yourself safe Incase something happens to me. And to protect the pack" he said and my heart clenched at the thought of something happening to him. I nodded determined but then stopped.

"Edrick. I don't even know if I'm going to be Luna" I said and he growled at me making me flinch a little.

"Let's move on." He gritted out. I sighed and we began again. But this time he got some of his pack warriors to come and help.

"There are two men about to attack. They won't hurt you but they will pretend to attack you and they are more stronger than regular humans so you can attack them and they won't be hurt. But, you need to find where they are at and stop them before they attack you first" Edrick said and I nodded and listened. I turned around and kicked one guy and heard a groan and then I turned to my left and swung a punch into the air.

"She throws a very good punch for a human Alpha" the warrior I was trying to attack said and the other guy groaned and I turned around to face him.

"Does a pretty good kick too" the other guy said in pain. I gasped and did my best to help the man up saying sorry. He laughed and patted my shoulder.

"It's ok Luna" he laughed. Edrick growled and they stopped laughing and became serious while I stiffened.

"Let's do it again" he said and I nodded while the two warriors said,"yes Alpha" at the same time.

"Now. Evangeline. This time they will be pretend to capture you but they won't hurt you at all I promise. You have to act quick. Werewolves have a step up from you so you'll have to be cautious" he said and I nodded and heard hem I quickly tried to grab one of the guys arms guis failed then I tried to kick the other one but ended up failing when he grabbed my leg and twisted behind my back. Not hurting me but showing me he could easily win this fight.

"That's enough for today. We should get you back home" Edrick said dismissing the two warriors and taking me home. ***Ok. This is not intended to be rude or anything at all. But I am not personally blind and I do not know what it is like. And if you guys don't understand why Evangeline is like this I mean don't read this book if you don't like it. I'm not forcing you to read it. Evangeline has never been able to do things by herself because of her family spoiling her and watching her 24/7. Just understand that I've never dealt with blindness. So writing this book is new for me so please don't be rude in the comments. Please and thank you. Love you my magical sea unicorns!

I don't have any questions do you all may ask!

Chapter 12- "What's going on?"

Jake's PovThe last week or two Evangeline has been sneaking out and coming to school the very next morning. I trust Evangeline, so I don't ask her what's going on and the past few weeks she has been walking around herself. Like. She doesn't need me to walk her around anymore. Well in the house and stuff but when she is at school she still needs a little help. But she couldn't learn all that herself? Could she? The weird thing is that her scent is different. Not to be weird or anything. I just doesn't smell like her usual flower perfume.

"Hey little one" I said warily looking at the back of her head. She was talking to Edrick.. Like always.. Evangeline and I's relationship have been a little rocky over the past few weeks. I heard a quiet growl and I knew it came from Edrick.

"Hey Jake" she said smiling. I smiled sadly at her knowing she couldn't see me. Edrick looked at me and I looked at him for a split second until looking back at her. She is so beautiful. I know I'm going to have to let her go though.. I can't do that to someone. I can't...

"Jake? Are you ok?" She asked and I let tears fill my eyes up as I brought her into a hug and stuffed my face into her hair covered shoulder sniffing in her scent.

"Yea I'm fine" I said and pulled away to see her face with a small frown. I frowned myself and took my thumb and pinkie from my right hand and made her smile making me smile once again.

"You should never frown" I said and she smiled and pecked my lips getting an immediate response. I heard a loud growl and then bones cracking which made me flinch but I pulled away from Evangeline and we walked to class. I just want to hold onto her for a little while longer. Just a few weeks longer.

You know we can't take Edrick's mate away from him. We already know how much it hurts to lose one.. my wolf Trent whimpered. I nodded my head and hid my scent making me smell like a human to all of the werewolves. I know Trent but she makes me calm.. She is the only good thing in my life ever since Heather... I said to my wolf making him growl at saying our dead mates name he retreated into my mind blocking me. I sighed and the day begun. After school Evangeline disappeared once again. I shifted and ran into the woods following her scent because I was done. I wanted to know where she was off to. I came into a opening and I saw Evangeline in work out clothes and two wolves I'm assuming warriors training her while Edrick watches. I came out of the woods in my wolf form and growled.

"Rouge" Edrick growled and went next to Evangeline whispering into her ear making me grow louder. His eyes glazed over before shifting into his huge black wolf and my dark brown wolf a few inches shorter than him. The warriors took Evangeline and me and Edrick fought.

"Who are you rouge!?" Edrick asked in his wolf form. I stood my ground and shook my fur looking at him with pure hate. The only reason was because of my wolf hating him for taking Evangeline from us. Trent treated Evangeline like his mate even though Heather couldn't be replaced Evangeline made us feel secure. I attacked him again and we stayed like that until I knocked him down and ran. Edrick is an Alpha I shouldn't be messing with him, he's also a hybrid and that even worse. I masked my scent once again and started heading home and walked into the from door making Sam, Natasha, and Ben gasp and Lily run under a couch.

"Jake? What happened?" Natasha asked and I snorted and ran up stairs to my room and shifted back into my human form then out on some clothes heading back down stairs.

"What's going on?" Sam asked and I looked at her and looked at Ben and Natasha. How do I tell them their daughter is mated to the highest ranked and King of the whole vampire and werewolf community and that he is also a Alpha and hybrid. I signed and told them to sit down.

"Well. I know where Evangeline is going now"

"Really? Where?"

"She is being trained to take care of herself by her mate... The king over all werewolf and vampire community, an Alpha, and he's a hybrid. Does that ring a bell?" I said and they all gasped and I nodded my head running my hands through my hair.

"Edrick Evans...." Sam said breathless and Natasha and Ben looked in deep thought.

"You know, the vampires are thinking about to war with us werewolves. Hopefully Edrick will make a good leader and make everything better" Ben said and I nodded and put my head in my hands thinking about if Evangeline will be happy with Edrick. I heard someone sit behind me and shoo the other two out of the room and I instantly knee who it was.

"Honey. I'm sorry this had to happen after... You know" Natasha said and I nodded looking up and into her eyes. Surprisingly Evangeline had all of her mother. Tears built up into my eyes and I let them freely fall and Natasha pulled me into a hug comforting me.

"Shh shh it's ok. Maybe things will look brighter in the future" she said rubbing my back after about an hour or so we pulled away and she got a tissue and wiped my tears from my cheeks and patted them.

"Now. Go upstairs and rest" she said and I nodded and thanked her silently. She nodded as I walked up stairs Lily hot on my tracks. Oh Evangeline, it's going to be hard letting you go...   ***Poor Jake.
Also the reason Jake and Sam smelt weird to Edrick was because they are werewolves trying to mask their scent! Jake and Sam were never together behind Evangeline's back!

Who knew Jake was a werewolf?

Who knew her family was hiding all this from her?

What does that make Evangeline?

Chapter 13- Challenge

Evangeline's PovIt has been 3 weeks of me getting trained and I'm doing amazing. I missed Homecoming and Jake was upset and so was I but we had our own dance at our house with mom dad and Sam. It was fun. But during my training I took down 3 warriors and 4 in their wolf form. It is the weekend and I'm taking a break so I'm with my family. And they keep offering me a drink I used to drink all the time but now it taste awful so I refuse to drink it.

"Honey can you please just take a few sips of the drink?" Mom asked and I pushed the cup away from me and looked in my mom's directing and got up.

"Mom I don't want to. It has an awful taste" I said and walked to the living room where Sam, dad, Lily, and Jake were. I went over to Jake and sat next to him.

"Hello little one" he said sadly. He's been like this the past few weeks and it's staring to scare me. I honestly love Jake. I really do but ever since I started training with Edrick I've grown stronger feelings for him than I ever had. And it makes me feel awful because I don't know what to do.

"Hey Jake" I said and I felt his hand on my leg rubbing circles around it and I felt a little weird because it wasn't Edrick's hand but I dismissed that thought and we all talked. Then we all heard a huge bang and growls. I got up and we all ran to the back and I heard growls and barks of wolfs. I snarled back in a human way but it oddly sounded like a wolf. I ignored it and grabbed a mop napping it making it into a stick.

"Rouges..." my mom whispered and I looked towards her and she whimpered.. What? They know? Are they?

"I'm sorry little one" Jake said behind me and I heard cracks of bones and three wolves past me and started to fight. I gasped and stood shocked until I heard a wolf charge towards me so I yelled and attacked stabbing the wolf in the side. It went like that until I heard a huge deadly growl. Everyone stopped and I heard a few wolves whimper and hide behind me and I was assuming it was my parents and Jake.

"Edrick" I said feeling his presence and I heard a low growl to show me he was here. Edrick must of saw my family behind me because he growled not knowing their sent's and seeing as they were rouges.

"Stop! This is my family" I said and Edrick growled at someone and the other growled back. I felt a nudge as my hand and I opened my palm and they rubbed their head into my head. I knew it was Jake and Edrick growled at an unmated male touching me in an affectionate way. Jake growled back and Edrick growled back and I heard more bones crack and my parents were still behind me and Jake left.

"Oh my God.." Mom said and I looked towards her.

"What?"

"Jake is challenging Alpha Edrick" she said and I gasped and felt an earth shattering growl and that could have only come from Edrick. I got my stick and before they could hurt each other I knocked them each back but not enough to hurt.

"Stop this!" I yelled and I felt something in me pulse. It was strong and my parents starting yelling at me and Jake and Edrick barked. I felt the ground come from underneath me and I was floating. I felt like something was changing it was weird and an awful feeling. I started to scream and my parents, Edrick, and Jake started freaking out.

Then everything blacked out.

I woke up in a hospital bed and I kept my eyes closed because it was no use. I sighed and then heard shuffling next to me.

"Vasílissa mou? Are you awake?" I heard a voice I recognized as Edrick day and I nodded and he said something under his breath.

"Open your eyes" he said and I sighed and opened my eyes up and I saw him. I saw Edrick's face. I can see him. I can see?

"I- I... I can s-see?" I said and Edrick sighed and some people walked in and you could feel power radiating off of them so I assume these are the elders Edrick was taking about.

"Miss. Rose. We have some news for you. Not only can you see now. You are a very important person" one said and I looked at them and at Edrick.

"What are they talking about?" I asked and I thought for a minute if my parents and family are werewolves that means I'm a werewolf. But I never felt anything Edrick says werewolves feel. No super senses or a wolf.

"Wait. That means I'm a werewolf? But I can't be. I've never had super senses or a wolf" I said and the elder looked at each other and handed me a cup of something and it looked like the drink mom wanted me to drink. I looked at it for a few more minutes and back at the elders.

"This drink stopped you from communicating with your wolf and stopped you from having any super senses. And Evangeline your not a normal werewolf" another said and I looked at them strangely. What do they mean I'm not a regular werewolf? Do I not have a wolf?

"Honey. Do you remember me?" One asked and she put her hands on my face and remember her. She's the woman who spoke in a foreign language and helped me. I nodded and she smiled shooing Edrick from his spot and taking it. She held my hand and I looked at her, Edrick, the other elders, and back at her.

"W-what am I" I asked with a shaky voice and she smiled and played with my hair tucking a strand of hair behind me ear.

"You're the Moon Goddess daughter. You are the one sent here to save us all" ***Dun dun dunnnnn. And guys of this book is going a little fast I'm sorry. Most of my books are usually 30 chapters or more but I'm making this book about 25 or so. Love you my magical sea unicorns!

How will Evangeline deal with this?

What will she say to her family?

What will happen between Jake and Edrick?

Chapter 14- No Boys

Evangeline's PovI looked at the woman blankly and started to laugh. I laughed so freaking hard I had to hold my stomach and take deep breaths. Edrick, the woman, and the other elders looked at me like I was crazy and I stopped and wiped my tears away looking at her. She had a serious face on making me sober up.

"You're kidding? Right?" I asked and she sighed and shook her head no. I let out a strangled breathe and motioned Edrick to come closer to me. He did and I fisted his shirt into my hands, he saw my distress and growled at everyone to get out. They all bowed their heads and went out. He climbed into bed with me and pulled me to his chest making tingles spread everywhere. I sighed in content and snuggled closer to him making his grip on my tighter.

"How did this happen?" I asked and I laughed humorless and shook my head. "No. Why did this happen?" I asked myself when Edrick kissed my head making me think. I have a boyfriend I have Jake. Why am I doing this? I'm an awful person.. Jake doesn't deserve this. Neither does Edrick.... I have to figure out all of this before I even think about boys.

"Edrick. You're going to have stay away from me. Like we can't do things like this." I said and he pulled back to look at me. He was mad. Not even mad he was fuming.

"What do you mean Evangeline? You mean I can't even be with my mate!? Is that what you mean!?" He asked yelling making me flinch a little. Then there was a bang on the door and Jake was there. I pushed Edrick away and told him to stand with Jake. He growled loudly making Jake growl at him for growling at me.

"Both of you shut up!" I yelled making them both go quiet.

"Now. With all that's happening I don't know how to handle everything with you guys. Jake you are my boyfriend and Edrick you are my mate. And all of this is stressing me. I can't deal with it. So Edrick we will still train but we can't do things like mates do. Jake I think we should take a break but with everything I can't deal with a boyfriend and a mate. I have to focus on me. I hope you both understand" I said and Edrick was fuming but Jake had a small sad smile. Jake nodded in understanding and Edrick growled loudly and shifted into his wolf running off.

"Hey. It's ok. I understand. I understand that you are going through something rough and need to focus on things. But Evangeline. I know you and Edrick are mates. Mates love each other dearly and were made for each other by the Moon Goddess herself. No matter what I will always love you. But I want you to pick Edrick after all this is over" he said and I smiled at Jake. This is why I fell in love with him. Not because of his looks. And of course I couldn't see him but he is handsome. Really. But I love him for his good heart. But all good things have to come to an end..

"Thank you so much Jake. I will always love you" I said and he smiled at me sadly and walked to the door.

"I love you too little one.." he said before walking out. I sighed and then someone else of course walked in. It was the doctor. Great. I have questions about all this anyway.

"Hello Miss. Rose. So to explain what was happening is that your family made you drink a type of drink making you unable to be a normal werewolf. After a few days you'll get enhanced hearing smelling speed and things of that nature. Then your wolf will reach out to you and try to talk to you. Your first shift may happen in a few days, weeks. It depends on when your wolf is ready" he said answering all my questions I nodded and he smiled.

"Thank you for telling me. Do I get to name my wolf or does she have her own name?" I asked and the doctor looked at me and laughed a little.

"Your wolf has her own name. When she begins to talk to you she will tell you" he said getting medication ready for me. He walked over and handed me a small pill and a glass of water.

"Here. You will have to take this one pill every day" he said and I nodded my head and said thank you. He gave a small nod and walked out while I took my pill.

Hello! I coughed on my own spit and shook my head and looked around the room.

I would appreciate it if you listened to me, my name is Amber! I'm your wolf! My so called wolf said in my head. Amber. That's a nice name. I concentrated hard and I saw her. It was the golden wolf I saw in my dream.

Hey! I remember you! Oh. How are you? Are you ok? I asked and I heard her laugh and it was he most angelic thing I have ever heard.

Yea I'm fine. Where you kept drinking that drink I was unable to communicate with you and I was chained up. Then there was a slither of a chance

I could reach out to you and I did in your dream! And I nodded my head in understanding.

I'm glad your ok! So do you wanna get to know each other? I asked and she laughed so hard I thought she would pass out. She fell on her side and after she was done she rubbed her paws over her snout.

Hun! I've known you since you were born! I just couldn't talk to you! She laughed

Well then I can get to know you! And we talked to hours!
***Sorry for long update! I've been busy my magical sea unicorns! I hope you liked it!

So she broke it off between Jake and Edrick?

How do you guys think they are doing?

What do you guys think of Amber?

Chapter 15- Shifting

Evangeline's Pov It's been a few days and I'm out of the infirmary. Edrick and I still practice everyday and everyday he makes it harder and harder. He is still really mad about everything so he is ignoring me. Jake is taking it fine he still talks to me as a friend. But my training begins in a few minutes so I should start getting ready. I put a black sports bra on and black leggings with my Nikes and headed out. When I went to the place we work out no one was there except one of the house pack warriors. I can sense he is one of the high ranked warriors.

Let's fight him. See if we can take him on. Amber said and I nodded and went up to him.

"Excuse me" I said and he turned around and his eyes widened and he bowed his head showing his neck a little submitting to me.

"Yes Luna" he said and I sighed and put my hand on his shoulder making him look up a little but not directly into my eyes.

"Call me Evangeline. But can we fight?" I asked making him look at me with wide eyes. I gasped and slapping my hand onto my head.

"Not like that! I mean as in training. I'm training with my new found skills. So maybe we can fight?.. You seem like a good opponent" I said and he nodded. I smiled and we got into a stance.

"Oh. And you can shift if you want to" I said making him nod. I smiled and we began I ran at him and he got ready but didn't expect me to slide under his legs and quickly hit at his back trying to find a weak point. He turned back to me and swung at me legs making me fall. I took that time and grabbed his foot and twisted it backwards making him fall.

His weak spot is shoulder. Before we started he kept rubbing it. Amber said making me nod at him and where I was distracted talking to her he flipped me over trying to punch my face. I dodge his punches. He got up shifting quickly. Now this may be tricky. He charged at me making me jump over him and riding him. He jerked and I ignited my canines and bit his shoulder making him yell. I didn't bit him hard enough to make him bleed out. But I did to where he gave the fight up. He whimpered and submitted. I got up and he shifted. I offered my hand and he smiled at me while his wound healed.

"You are doing great Lu- I mean, Evangeline" he said bowing and walking off. I sighed running my hands threw my hair and then saw Edrick. He looked shocked and proud.

"Hey Edrick... How long have you been standing there?" I asked taking deep breaths.

"I saw everything. Your doing great. And-" he was cut off by my screaming. There was a burning in my body and I felt my bones move and shift around making it agonizingly painful.

"Evangeline! Oh God. You're shifting. I'm going to carry you to the woods. Ok?" He said softly at the end rubbing my back. I saw Edrick's family and mine run out staring at me. Edrick picked me up and carried me into the woods. He laid me down on the sold grass next to a stream making soothing sounds.

"E-Edrick it-it hur-ts" I whimpered while Amber tried to push threw. He coed at me calming me down a little and I let a scream out while it turned into a howl. While fur sprouted fast and bones cracked into new places. I closed my eyes and when I opened them back up everything was more advanced. I looked around and found Edrick's wolf. He gave me a wolfie smile making me stick my tongue out.

You look beautiful. He said through mind link I got up and trotted over to the stream looking at myself. I was a beautiful golden wolf with vibrant blue eyes. I've still gotten used to having my eye sight back so my wolf eye sight just made it worse but it's so cool! I love it! I looked over at Edrick and pounced in him catching him off guard. I licked his check making him purr, I pulled away and tilted my head.

I didn't know wolves could purr I laughed in our mind link making him roll his eyes getting up with me. I jumped all over the place excited. This is very new for me. What I'm a talking about? Everything about these past few months have been new! Werewolves! Mates! Packs! Rouges! Elders! Being able to see! Being the Moon Goddess' child! Being someone who is supposed to save everyone!

You ok? Edrick asked coming up beside me nudging me a little. I nodded my head and sniffed my way back to the pack house letting Edrick follow behind me wondering what my sudden mood swing was about. I scratched the door until Zoey opened it and gasped. I walked in and my family and Edrick's gasped and gawked at my golden wolf. Amber was soaking up the attention but I was still thinking hard. I went up the stairs and to my room that I switched to. I shifted and put on some comfortable clothes and crawled into bed.

"Today's been a long day..." I sighed to myself. I rolled over to look out the window. I closed my eyes and sighed. Ah. Darkness. One of the many things I'm very familiar with. And oddly the one thing I'm the most comfortable with. I sighed and scrunched my eyebrows together opening my eyes back up. When I did I saw someone out my window smiling a sinister smile at me. I gasped but before I could scream he opened the window and attacked me. ***Hey my magical sea unicorns! This is the fastest update I've done in a while! But, I'm very truly sorry if this book is going really fast! I don't want the book to be that long and I'm running out of things for it. And I'm trying really hard. I hope you all understand!

Evangeline'a wolf is gold, what does this mean?

Is Evangeline going to be ok with all that's happening? Or will the anxiety and stress get to her?

Who is the person who attacked her?

Chapter 16- Attack

Evangeline's PovI shifted into my wolf while the intruder did the same thing. We were circling each other. And I realized I was in the pack house. A lot of pack members live here. I'm there Luna.. I can't put their lives in danger. I growled at the guy and ran out of my room and down stairs while he followed behind me. Edrick saw and he shifted too. I ran outside and deep into the woods. My parents, Edrick's family, Jake, and Edrick's friends were following behind. I stopped and looked at the wolf.

Who are you and what are you doing on my territory?! I asked him in a mind link. He let a a growl that sounded like a chuckle and circled me.

Calm down there little girl. I'm here for my Alpha. He wants you. He heard the Blind Beauty has risen. You probably don't even know why you're important he laughed and Edrick and Jake growled in warning but Edrick's was louder.

I do. I know I'm supposed to save everyone from something. I said knowing my knowledge. And he laughed and shook his head.

Dear. Did you know you have powers? Probably not. You are supposed to stop my Alpha. But I doubt that. I mean, look at you! He laughed making me growl and jump onto him attacking him. He tried to big my neck but

I dodged him and but his hind leg making him yelp and snap at my face. I backed away quickly and went around him bitting his side. He growled at me and bit my leg I barked at him making him growl. I growled lowly at and he snarled and snapped at him while we circled each other. I stood my ground and Amber spoke to me.

Listen carefully Evangeline. I want you to close your eyes and focus on someone or something you love. I suggest mate. But I know how you feel about that. Think about our family. And when it gets overwhelming open your eyes and attack. She said and I nodded I closed my eyes and heard the wolf growl. I thought about my family and how much I love them. After a minute I opened my eyes and attacked the wolf. My fur was glowing and when I bit his side he yelped and it turned into an odd sound and he started to stiffen up and before I knew it he was just a gold statue. My eyes widened as I looked at the statue and I looked back at my family and friends and they were all in shock. I whimpered and ran away. All of this is too overwhelming.. What else can I do?

Are you ok? Amber asked and I nodded and she saw how much I didn't feel like talking so she went to the back of mind and stayed quiet. I walked until I was by a stream. I huffed and laid down on the ground watching as the stream flowed. I heard twigs snap behind me so I popped up and growled and I saw a small brown wolf, a yellow one, and a dark brown one. It's Zoey, Max, and Sam. I got up and backed away from them. I'm scared I'll hurt them. I don't wanna hurt my sister, my mates friend and sister. They came forward with their heads down. I shook mine and ran away while they chased after me.

Leave me alone! I don't wanna hurt any of you! I yelled at them throw mink link.

Let me take over Amber said and I nodded while she took over. She stopped and looked at them and they stopped, Amber gave a warning growl at them making them step back a little.

I understand you all are worried about Evangeline but you all need to back off! She needs time to process all this by herself! Don't follow us! She growled at them and ran off somewhere. I am thankful of Amber. I finally have someone to talk to that I can fully trust.

Thank you Amber I said and she nodded and put her snout in the air and sniffed she growled and turned around seeing something move. She sniffed one more time and I let myself smell it to. Fresh pine and cinnamon.... Edrick..

Come out. Amber said trying to be closed off to her mate. She knew I didn't want anyone bothering me and she's protecting me even from our mate.

Amber. Please let me talk to Evangeline he said and she growled at him and he cautiously walked up to her and rubbed his face into the side of hers. She purred and I watched, I really don't want to be bothered right now but Amber is enjoying herself. Amber knocked out of it and growl at him making him back up and lay down showing us submission. Amber was proud at making an Alpha show submission but she was also sad that he did. I took back control and went up to Edrick and tucked myself into his side, trying to seek comfort he saw this and moved so we were facing each other. I tucked my head into his neck and laid his head on the side of mine licking my fur. I purred finding comfort.

Why are you so complicated? Edrick asked me and I pulled my head from his neck and looked at me.

I don't know. I've always been like that. If you don't like it, suck it up I said and he let a wolfie laugh out and licked my cheek laying his head back on mine making me close my eyes and purr again.

I don't like it Evangeline. I love it. He said and I gave him a wolfie smiled and I laid my head down on his paws and he laid his on top of mine. I purred while he licked my ears making them twitch. We both fell asleep right there.   ***Hello my magical sea unicorns! I have just uploaded a new book! It's a humor/love book so make sure to go check it out! Thank you guys!

Who is happy Edrick and Evangeline are getting along?

What else can Evangeline do?

Who is the wolf's Alpha?

Chapter 17- Important Plans

Evangeline's Pov The last few days I've been practicing and seeing what other powers I have. I can control the elements as in nature, water, fire, and wind, then I can control wolves by bitting them, people I can also but my eyes glow when I look at them controlling them, and turn them into golden statues. But only if I'm thinking of something I love dearly! And I can control it. And I'm wondering if I can reverse it but I'll try that another day. The rest of my powers I don't know yet but I'm still trying. I'm actually training with Edrick right now.

"Evangeline I need you to concentrate" he said and I huffed while in my wolf form and trying to practice my powers. I snarled at him the ground began to shake. What the... He quickly jumped from where he was and the ground cracked open I shook my head. I stumbled back a little bit and looked at Edrick shifting back into my human form and putting on shorts and a sports bra n real quick.

"I almost killed you....." I said looking at him. He shook his head and stepped towards me, grabbing me by the arms towards him.

"You didn't mean to. I'm fine. See? I didn't get any scratches" he said and I nodded while looking at the hole while he hugged me. I made it go away and I sighed, well I have another power down and I feel like that's the last one. I saw Sam walking towards us with someone with her, Zoey and Mason where trailing behind laughing at something.

"Hey Eve! I want you to meet my mate! Ethan I just met him today!" Sam said and I looked over Ethan. He seems like a very relaxed kind of guy. I smiled at him and he gave me a boyish grin.

"Hello Ethan" I said and stuck my hand out for him to shake but he bowed his head at me and submitted.

"Hello Luna" he said so I grabbed his hand and shook it laughing making his head jerk up a little.

"Come on! You don't have to call me Luna! Call me Evangeline!" I said and he looked up at me and smiled and nodded towards Edrick.

"Hey Evangeline, I also wanted to introduce you to my mate Mason. And you already know I'm Edrick's little sister. Zoey. But I'm the cooler one of course" she said flipping her hair making me laugh.

"Hello Mason and I totally agree Zoey" I said and she laughed with me making Edrick grumble under his breath.

"Well as you can see we all have our mates so why not go out on a triple date?" Zoey asked looking at Edrick and I, Edrick slipped his hand around my waist pulling me into his chest. I felt tingles all over my body making me think about Edrick and I... In hot scenarios.... Edrick growled smelling my aroused body.

"We can't. We have our own plans" he said and they nodded their heads walking off. I looked at Edrick and slapped his chest.

"We do not! You just didn't want to go!"

"No. We actually have somewhere to be. Now that your Luna and Queen of all supernaturals we have to deal with things. The rouges have found vampire rouges and apparently they are plotting to get you so we need to go" he said straining himself from going off on me. I whimpered in my head and nodded with all seriousness. He nodded back and told me to go clean up in nice clothes, we have to go to another pack to discuss it. I went to my room and saw a dress with heels, I shook my head while smiling.

"Oh Edrick..." I said and picked the dress up and walked to the bathroom. I took a shower to get all the sweat off of me and when I got out I let my hair dry to it's natural straight hair. I slipped the dress on with the shoes, I put on mascara and winged eyeliner. I smiled at myself and walked out, down stairs Edrick was pacing in a suit. I smiled at his form, he looked so stressed and worried, I guess he heard me because he looked in my direction and smiled grabbing my hand and walking to a limo.

"To the Red Blossoms Pack please" Edrick said to our driver and he nodded. I smiled and looked around the limo in awe. As the driver rolled up the window making us invisible to him Edrick grabbed me and sat me on his lap while he snuggled his head into my neck.

"I've been waiting so long for me to be able to do this" he said and I laughed pushing him away making him growl as I sat back where I previously was.

"Edrick remember I said no doing this. I let you the day of the attack because I need to calm down. It's not fair to Jake" I said and he growled putting me back on his lap but making me straddle him this time.

"I shouldn't have to wait for my mate. And it especially should be fair. I'm your mate not Jake" Edrick said in a strained voice, I sighed and sat my hand on his check while he snuggled onto it savoring the tingles and the warmth of his mates hand.

"I know.. I will pick you in the end, I always will. But you have to under-stand all this is hard for me and to let my first love go" I said and he growled opening his eyes that were pitch black... Oh no... His wolf is out.

"Hello baby" his wolf said and held my waist tightly making me blush as my dress rid up as his hands touched my thighs.

"H-hello Caden" I said and he groaned as I felt something poke me making me gasp and get off of his lap from the extreme tingles. He smirked at me then pinched my cheek and gave me a lopsided smile.

"You're so cute my mate" he said and I smiled at him. We talked un-til we got to Red Blossoms Pack House. Caden is so goofy and sweet. ***I'm so sorry my magical sea unicorns! I have been busy with everything! And winter guard just started today! And I'm really excited! I love you all! Oh and again the reason Jake and Sam smelt weird to Edrick a few chapters back was because they were werewolves trying to mask their scent! Jake and Sam were never together behind Evangeline's back!

How will the meeting go?

Who thought Sam was with Jake behind Evangeline's back?

Who is trying to get Evangeline?

Chapter 18- Meeting

- -

Evangeline's PovWhen we walked in Edrick had his arm securely around me as I saw people staring at me. Men with lust and attraction while women had envy and curiosity. But I think everyone was curious about the blind human girl who got her eye sight back and is actually a werewolf and not even that, the Moon Goddess' daughter. We went into the office and Edrick and I went to the very end where the King and Queen were supposed to sit at. It made me anxious from sitting there and so many people staring. Then is began.

"So. We are gathered her today because of my Queen receiving empty threats and her being the women from the prophecy. Now let's begin" Edrick said as everyone sat down. All the highest Alpha and Luna's from their countries and states staring at me.

"My King. I am not trying to disrespect you at all but your Queen is making a huge problem for all werewolves and creatures because of who she is. Especially her being the Queen" one Alpha said and Edrick nodded his head trying to stay calm.

"I understand that Alpha Daniel but she is your Queen and no matter what you will learn to deal with these problems as we are trying to find a solution and of course she is mew to all of this because of her family"

"That's Just it My king! Your Queen is causing us too many problem for us to deal with! We have packs of our owns dealing with enough and then she comes! Also she doesn't know what the heck she is doing! I say we find a new Queen who knows what she is doing and that doesn't cause us problems!" Another Alpha said making the whole room erupted in mumbles. Edrick stood up and let a giant roar making everyone silent, his eyes were darker than usual showing he was fighting control of his wolf.

"Alpha Trent! If you say something like that again about your Queen again I will end your life in front of your own pack! And I don't think the Moon Goddess would be very happy of the way you're talking about her daughter!" Edrick roared making the Alpha whimper and submit to him while his Luna rubbed his arm comforting him. She looked at me and silently apologized with her eyes. I nodded towards her telling her it was ok.

"Now. I understand that you all are going through problems and some may be caused by my Queens appearance. But, we are figuring it out. And if you all wait we will be able to fix all of your problems. But do not take it out on your Queen. Now I want her to say a few words on the matter and if she would like, you all can ask questions if she is comfortable with it" Edrick said and I nodddd standing up while he sat down. I looked at all the curious eyes as I took a deep breath.

"Hello everyone. My name is Evangeline Rose. As you all know I was a blind human before. But then I soon got my eye sight back from my mother The Moon Goddess. Then figured out I was a wolf like all of you. I'm so very sorry if I have made any problems for you all but I'm trying to resolve the problem and trying to figure out what I'm supposed to do. I'm working and training everyday to help and strengthen me to be ready for anything. But I will not fail my citizens. Because if I am Queen I will do anything to protect all of you. I will put my own life before yours. Because I will not watch my citizens die and get hurt for something that is cause by me. And whatever I need to do I will do it. And I have my own pack and I now how it feels to be under pressure but that will not stop me from protecting all of you." I said and sat back down while Edrick looked at me proudly. I held my breath as everyone stared at me and slowly stared clapping. I gave a small smile knowing that I was accepted. These are my people and I will make sure I protect them with everything o have in me.

"Now. On the matter of my Queen. She is the one from the prophecy. The one who is supposedly save all supernatural kind. It says a great darkness will take over and kill everyone until they have control over all super-naturals promising misery. But one woman a very special woman called the Blind Beauty will stop this but she will have to sacrifice something she loves dearly. And that woman is your Queen Evangeline. We do not know who the people are yet but we are trying to get to the bottom of it." Edrick said making everyone and there was one person eyes making me feel uncomfortable I looked around until I landed on a figure but they quickly left. I shook my head and looked back at everyone.

"My King. Could it be rouges?" A Luna asked and he looked thoughtful.

"Yes. We did discuss that and there is a high chance of it being rogues, but we do not officially know yet because we found tools around our territory covered in wolfsbane. And rouges have no reason to use that" Edrick said and everyone nodded thinking.

"My King?"

"Yes Luna Sydney?"

"Could the rouges be.... Be..." Luna Sydney said pausing looking at her hands then at her mate and back at Edrick and I. "Be working with.... Zane?" She asked and Edrick's eyes darkened while I looked at him confused. Who's Zane? Is he someone important? Bad? Good? I don't know..

"Yes. My King and Queen. There's a high chance it could be Zane. He's always wanted power and he's always been so greedy" An Alpha said then Edrick got up storming out.

"Everyone is dismissed we will reschedule this meeting once Edrick calms down. Thank you all for coming" I said and they all bowed and started leaving while I ran after Edrick. ***Hope you all liked this chapter! Oh and please go check out my other book Mystical and Mysterious and maybe the sequel Mysterious Attitude? M&M is on my page and the other is on my other page

Did you all like this chapter?

What will Evangeline have to give up?

Who is Zane?

Chapter 19- Unexpected Guests

Evangeline's Pov I walked into mine and Edrick's room after riding home in an empty limo by myself. I saw him pacing the room trying to calm himself down. I sighed as I walked over to him and laid my hand on his back.

"Hey, are you ok?" I asked and he spun around not knowing it was me about to yell. I flinched when he glared at me, when he saw it was me his eyes softened and he sighed pulling me to his chest breathing in my scent calming himself down.

"I'm sorry. I just. I lost it when they kept blaming you for everything and then Zane.... And I... I"

"Shh. Edrick it's fine" I said and we looked into each others eyes, I won't bother him about who Zane is right now. I lead him to bed and sat him down making him lay down. I crawled in bed beside him but he had different plans as he pulled me on top of him making me look into his eyes. I gasped at he lashed his hands on my hips and started to his my neck. I moaned as a got to a certain spot between my neck and shoulder. He growled and I felt his canines rub against the spot. I knew what he wanted to do so I gave him more access to my neck while moaning. He stopped and pulled away so he could look me in the face.

"Are you sure?" He asked huskily making me more aroused. I nodded my head eagerly and pulled his head back down to my neck. He growled in pleasure in my ear before biting down on my neck making me gasp and wiggle in pain. He held me in place while his teeth were still in me, soon an immense amount of pleasure hit me making me moan load and hold onto him. He pulled me back down where u was laying on his chest and ran his hand through my hair smelling it.

"Go to sleep Vasílissa mou" He said and u fell into a deep sleep with a smile on my face.

—5 months later—It's been a few months after Edrick marked me.. And I also convinced Edrick to let Lilly come to live with us instead of with my parents and Jake. I've missed my Lilly and I'm so happy I have her back with me. Edrick gets jealous with how much she gets attention. Also Edrick has been very possessive after he marked me, more than usual. Jake was happy for me but I could see the sadness in his eyes and I hugged him while telling him we will always be close to each other no matter what. I've gotten all my powers mainly down. Controlling the elements, turning people into gold statue, making my eyes glow letting me see into their minds and thoughts, and last but not least I can control others with me bitting them in wolf form and in human form I just stare into their eyes.

"Hey Eve, have you seen Ethan?" Sam asked walking into the living room and I shook my head no making her sigh and sit next to me exhausted, while laying her head on my shoulder.

"He's been so busy. With being top warrior and him training everyone and Zoey is the female beta helping Beta Mason. Then you have to worry about your powers, people wanting to kidnap up, you being the Moon Goddess' daughter. And on top of all that you are the Luna of this back and Queen of all supernaturals!" She said in one breathe and I laughed lightly at the end of her story.

"I'm sorry Sam. I've just been so caught up with everything. Why don't we have a day just to ourselves? Huh?" I said and she sat up and pulled me out the door with her making me laugh. But we didn't get two steps out when alarms went off and everyone started to flee. I looked around and saw a little girl being chased by a rouge. I pushed Sam into the house knowing she is an omega and shifted into my wolf not caring about my clothes and attacking the wolf. I bit him and made him attack some of his own while I nudged the little girl onto my back running her to the safe house.

I put her in and stood in front guarding it. A wolf was about to pounce on one of our warriors but I stared at him thinking of Edrick and him turned into a statue. The warrior looked at me and nodded while I did the same but someone rammed into my side making me roll over with the wolf. I snarled but stopped when I saw a beaten up Edrick. I whimpered and budged his snout with mine earning a pained whimper from him. I looked up and saw another wolf about the same size as me with a scar along his eye.

Hello sweetheart, it's nice to finally meet you the wolf said to me making me stand over Edrick in a protective way.

Who are you and why are you on my territory! I snarled at the wolf and he gave me a evil look making me scared but I didn't let him see that.

Well my name is Zane sweetheart. I'm assuming yours is Evangeline Rose? He said making my eyes widen a little. This is the guy. The guy I wanted to know about for months. Every time I would ask Edrick who is was he would change the subject or tell me not to worry about it. I looked at Edrick while he looked at me whimpering.

You know what Zane? I said and he tilted his head telling me to continue. I want you to get off of my territory and leave! I barked at him and he gave me a wolfie laugh and I watched at a very familiar wolf walked from behind him.

Derek...   ****tries to mumble something out*To tried to speak. Night Magical Unicorns! (It's like 1 in the morning where I am lolz)

inserts question

Chapter 20- Old Memories

Evangeline's Pov Derek.... What is he doing here?! He can't be here... He was in jail... He's a wolf?! Oh my lord all of this is messed up. He's supposed to be in prison! I wobbled a little and Edrick whimpered at me faintly licking my paw.

It's been forever my sweet. I've missed you, and I would advise you to tell that mutt to stop licking you Derek growled making me whimper from the memories.

Flashbacks—2 weeks after they moved—I went through the halls after class by myself hoping I could get to my classroom. We just moved here a couple of weeks ago from our old and may I say 6th house. Jake didn't get the chance to come get me cause I went out as soon as the bell rung and now I'm lost holding onto the walls for dear life. I bumped into another wall and cursed a little under my breath.

"Watch where your- oh I'm sorry. Are you new? Do you need help?" A male voice ask and rested his hands on my waist steadying me. I smiled and nodded my head and I heard him chuckle while grabbing my hand and leading me somewhere.

"So what's your name?"

"My name is Derek my sweet, what about you?" He asked making me blush and look down while he guided me.

"My name is Evangeline... Also I'm sorry you have to help me I tried to go out of my classroom by myself and.. You probably already saw my eyes.. I'm blind"

"It's totally fine. I'm glad I bumped into you" he said and we stoped somewhere while I looked around.

"I'll see you around my sweet.." he said kissing my neck and putting me at the door. I blushed and walked in holding onto the wall.

—2 weeks after they met—"Hey Evangeline! Hey Jake..." Derek said coming up to me and Jake while he said Jake's name with venom.

"Hey Derek!"

"Hey, Derek..."

"How are you my sweet?" Derek asked, Derek has been very nice and we became friends very quickly. I assumed we were at Jake's classroom caused he kissed my head and told me to be safe and let Derek take me.

"Bye!"

"Lets go Evangeline" Derek said pulling me close to his side possessively making me a little uncomfortableness try to create more space but just resulting in him pulling me closer.

"Don't ever pull away from me" he said and I whimpered and nodded my head while he took me to class.

—2 months later—"Derek please stop! Stop Derek! Derek I said stop!" I yelled and screamed after Derek pulled me into his car and drove off after he started a fight with Jake. I assume Derek punched Jake for kissing me. Taking my first kiss.

"You have to understand! You are mine! No one else's! Especially that mutt! You are mine Evangeline!" He yelled pulling me out and pulling me into a house taking me somewhere. He opened a door and pushed me onto a bed the I heard a loud thump making me realize he closed the door and locked it. Then I felt him crawl on top of me as start to assault me. Kissing my neck and ripping my clothes off. I heard him trying to take his belt off and that's when I struggled against him.

"Derek! Stop! Please don't do this! Stop! Stop now! St-" I was cut off when he slapped me making me cry harder.

—2 hours later- I ran out of Derek's house and tried to find help by screaming and crying covering my body with a piece of fabric. Someone came and helped me taking me to the police and they took me in for questioning.

"What happened sweetie" a nice female voice came into my hearing. I shook violently and started to cry while she came over and hugged me.

"H-he... h-e r-rap... rape..." I couldn't finish my sentence with out crying harder and she cooed at me and hugged me tighter and I visioned how I felt and started to scream and push her away.

"No! Don't touch me! P-please..." I said crying and she sighed and I could feel her body heat in front of me.

"Who was it"

"D-Derek Antonio.."_____________End of flashback

Evangeline... Are you ok?... Edrick asked through mind link and I whimpered backing a little away from Derek and Zane and closer to Edrick.

All the memories flashed in front of me at once making em whimper and shake.

I see you remember me my sweet Derek said chuckling making me growl at him and he growled back making me flinch a little. He wasn't supposed to be out... He can't be out..

If we haven't been formally introduced I'm Zane Evans. Edrick's brother that was supposed to be king but dad gave it to him. Also I am the Alpha of rogues he said smiling a wolfie smile at me making me cringe.

And don't try your powers on us they won't work. Also I'm helping Derek back get his property back. And he of course wants it back more knowing you are so much more important now he said making me growl loudly stopping everyone while they all looked at me.

I. Am. Not. Property! And you will not hurt my people and you will leave my territory now! I yelled and all the rogues left when Zane howled.

Would you like to say anything to Edrick? Derek said snarling our Edrick's name. I looked at him and laid softly on him licking behind his ear.

I love you so much Edrick... I love you so so much. I want to bear your pups. I want to stay with you forever I said in our mind link only.

I love you too Vasílissa mou Edrick said and I licked his ear again. Then I saw Jake's wolf pouncing onto Derek's making me bark then run towards Zane but then I saw Derek cut deep into Jake's stomach making him fall onto the ground.

Jake! No! I howled before feeling a pain in my side making em fall over seeing Jake on the ground not moving and Edrick barley breathing..

I love you guys...

I love you Edrick...   ***Ripppppp sorry
for the cliffhanger my beautiful magical sea unicorns! but you all got a fast
update! Yay!

Who though Zane would be Edrick's brother?

Who knew Evangeline went through that?

What will happen to Edrick and Jake?

Chapter 21- Hostage

Edrick's PovI saw them take my Evangeline right before I passed out. I woke up in a hospital bed with my family and Evangeline's dad looking at me, when he saw I was away he looked away while my family squealed at hugged me.

"Honey I'm so glad you're ok!" Mom screeched as she cried on my chest. Dad stood behind her and smiled at me.

"Son I'm sorry for ever thinking your mate was weak and unfitted to be a Luna. She's actually a strong woman" he said making me smile but frown when I remembered Jake getting injured.... Evangeline getting taken.... She said she loved me....

"Where's Evangeline?.... Is Jake ok?" I asked and my family's smiles soon went to frowns and I looked over to Ben, Evangeline's dad.

"They took her... They have her... Derek has her... Zane has her.... They are going to break her... A-and Jake..... Jakes in a coma!" Ben said falling to the ground and I assume his mate sensed his distress because soon Natasha was in here soothing him.

"I'll take him. We will get her back Edrick. I promise you that because when I find her I'm going to rip all those rogues limb from limb" she said walking out with a crying Ben. Now I know where Evangeline got her intimidation from. But of course the Moon Goddess gave that to her also.

"I have to go find her!....." I yelled trying to get out of bed but getting pushed down by Zoey with a stern look I growled and ripped the IV out of my wrist and groaned trying again.

"Edrick sit your butt down! I've been so worried about why dad has been so over edge and then why you started after you got Alpha and King position! But it was because of Zane and you didn't tell me?! Also you never told me about the war that might happen between the werewolves and vampires! I wouldn't mess with me right now!" Zoey yelled while Mason held her back trying to calm her down.

"You're sisters right Edrick. You didn't even tell us" Max said while Xan and Devon were beside her.

"You should have told us dude" Xan said giving me a disappointed look. While Devon just shook his head while his arms were folded in front of him.

I told you, you should have told her.Caden said giving me a wolfie smirk making me roll my eyes at him.

He's right. But that doesn't matter right now! We have to get to mate! Axel yelled making me nod and Caden growl while I let them take over control making me eyes black and my pupil red.

"Let us go! We need to save mate! She needs us! Now!" Caden and Axel yelled making them flinch and step back but the doctor came in and poked a syringe in my neck making me dizzy. I feel back in bed and tried to fight the darkness but it took over but not before Caden, Axel, and I called out to Evangeline.

"Vasílissa..... mou...."

Evangeline's PovHey you dummy get up! We have to get out of here! I heard a voice in my head say I groaned and knew it was Amber and got up looking at the chains around me. Silver with wolfsbane in it.... Why is it not hurting me?

Because our mother gave us the gift of being immune to wolfsbane and silver. Now come on! She yelled while I groaned getting up and tugging at the chains but failing and just falling back down in exhaustion.

"Oh look at you my sweet. Maybe I should make you even more exhausted" he said walking close to my cage. I shook in fear forgetting all about my training and powers and unconsciously blocked Amber.

"P-please d-d-don't hur-t me-me" I stuttered out shaking even more when he walked closer to me putting his filthy hands all over my body making me whimper.

"I won't do anything yet. But I will soon" he said waking back out letting Zane in making me cower to the corner. He smirked at me making me cringe.

"So your my brother's mate? You're very pretty and very strong for a little thing aren't ya. Not so brave now though, are ya sweetheart?" He said making me whimper and shake then yelp when he grabbed my by my upper arm pulling me up to his face.

"Derek and I are going to have so much fun with you. But first let's get down to business" he said dragging me out of the cell taking me somewhere.

"Derek and I both wanted you for pleasure but we soon figured of who you are. You're the blind beauty, daughter of The Moon Goddess. So we figured out something. If we use you to our advantage. You see Derek and

I are werewolves I have vampire on me like Edrick so I'm a hybrid. But we control rogues and we are allies with the vampires. Has Edrick told you about that?"

"N-no..."

"Well we want to take over the population of werewolves so we want to go to war with them. Edrick has been so stressed trying to keep it under control along with dear old father. But you, you are supposed to help keep the piece that's one of your destined quests. But have you ever heard how the prophecy goes?" He asked and I shook my head no. He laughed and began telling me what it was and how it went.

"Our land is full of mysterious things. But naked to the human eye is the side full of the most mysterious creatures. Werewolves, vampires, warlocks, hybrids, witches, and even more. They all lived in peace but the peace soon became havoc between werewolves and vampires making the rest of the creatures hide and cower away. Soon the Moon Goddess made a King and Queen to keep everything peaceful. But one day that will change and one of the sides will become greedy and want all power and declare war. But one day even if before or after the war, will arise The Blind Beauty. She is a gift from the Moon Goddess, her own daughter sent to help us all from the havoc and destruction. She will have to sacrifice something she loves dearly to do all of this but she, she is the key of holding peace between us all."   ***Well. Yay update! Lol. But. I'm honestly about to lose my crap because people are still commenting about Evangeline even after I put the note up and I am trying so hard not to us any bad words on here because I respect people who don't like it and oh my lord. I love you my magical unicorns!

You all can ask the questions this update! Because I'm generous not lazy!

Chapter 22- BrainWashed

Evangeline's Pov—3 months later—".... This is why we should take down the werewolves and over throw The King" I said while the vampires smiled with there fangs making me smile.

"How do we know we can trust you?" One of the vampire yelled from the crowd and I grabbed the mic and jumped off the stage in the middle of all them while Derek and Zane watched me.

"Because when we do I will kill the king and his family" I said smiling sinisterly making the vampires cheer.

Evangeline this isn't you please- Amber said making me block her out. She's been running my life for way to long ever since I got my eye sight back. It's now time for me to take that back. I walked over to Derek and Zane but when Derek reached for me I stepped back. W-what am I doing... T-this isn't me...

"Remember" Zane said pushing me towards Derek while all I felt was power and lust. I looked at Derek and he kissed me forcefully. I never liked him doing this he would rape me and touch me while Zane would so much as kiss me but that it. I felt disgusting. But I also needed it. Edrick will never be anything to me. And I will take over his kingdom but the only way is through Derek and Zane, so I have to go through this is I want to achieve what I want.

Edrick's PovIt's been months since I've last seen my beauty. I've only known my mate for a year and all of this happens. I'm sitting in the meeting hall with my dad while we try and make a plan to get her back. We've been trying to make a plan for months. I finally snapped.

"What is this? What are we doing? We've been in this dang room for months trying to make the perfect plan to get my mate back! Your Queen back! Months! Months trying to get this God dang plan together! Now make one today or I am going to find her myself!" I roared and stood up storming out. Everyone on there is a bunch of idiots.

"Son! Son!" My father called after me making me growl and turn twisted him my eyes red from blood list with Axel trying to take over control.

Let me take over! Now! Axel roared in my head baring his fangs while Caden snapped and snarled at him.

You need to calm down Axel! Look what you are doing to Edrick! Caden yelled making me grip my head at their annoying argument.

I don't care! Now let me have control! I growled loudly making me forcefully change a little showing my black eyes with red pupils, my fangs and canines growing out, and fur sprouting on my skin and it turning more pale.

Look what you are doing to him! He is stressing enough right now! And how do you think mate would react to this?! Caden snarled and Axel immediately stopped wondering and fearing about what Evangeline would think. I sighed and changed back while my father came up to my grabbing my shoulders.

"Son. Are you ok?" Dad asked making me whimper and shake my head. He pulled me into a hug and I cried on his shoulder thinking about what they are doing to my Evangeline. Jake is still in a coma and her family are trying to distance themselves from mine while mine is trying to help and I have to take care of Evangeline's yappy annoying dog Lily. Everything is just utter chaos. She is supposed to keep peace for us but she isn't here so everything is just falling apart.

"Dad what if they hurt her? What if she is dead? What will I do without her? What if-" I cried and dad pulled back and cut me off.

"Son what if the sky falls down and monkeys take over the world? If she wasn't alive you would be in so much pain. You marked her." He said and this is true but for some reason my mind link is blocked off from her and I can't feel anything except...

"Dad. They rape her! I know they do! I can feel it through our mark! That's the only thing I can feel and it kills me!" I cry and his eyes gloss over and mom comes in and cooes at me taking me in here arms.

"Mom. This is all my fault. I couldn't save her. I couldn't save her or Jake" I said and she shushed me.

"Edrick it isn't your fault. It's your brothers and Derek's. It's not your sweetie. I'm going to call Devon, Xan, and Max to come get you ok? Maybe you can go out and get your mind off everything while we make a plan" she said and I know I wouldn't be able to say anything cause she glared at me so I nodded. She wants me to go out because I've been in the meeting hall ever since Evangeline got taken.

"Now. Go wait down stairs while I mind link them to come" she said and I nodded going down stairs waiting in the living room.

"Hey Edrick" Max said with the guys behind her. She smiled at me sat next to me patting my back.

"What do you want to bro" Xan asked sitting on my other side patted my back in a friendly manner making me smile a little.

"Maybe go out and get frozen yogurt" I said and Devon nodded his head and threw my over his shoulder packing me to his car while Max and Xan laugh.

"This is how I get treated" I said and they all laughed as we get into his car and off to the human town to get frozen yogurt. Dad better have a plan to get Evangeline back when I get home. And if not I'm going out tonight by myself to get her.   ***Hello my magical sea unicorns! I hope you all like the update! And I posted a new book and I really feel good about this book so go check it out!

What will Evangeline do?

Will they make up a plan?

How will Edrick react when he sees Evangeline isn't in her right mind?

Chapter 23- War

Zane's PovShe is doing great... We have her wrapped around our fingers. She thinks a lot so she tries to break the brainwash spell we got a witch to put on her for us but all we have to say is remember and she is ok. We told her she can have all kinds of power from doing this and she was in. Today was the day. Today is the day we start the war and win. With Evangeline on our side we are sure we are going to win.

"Evangeline are you ready?" Derek asked and she nodded her eyes sparking with something deathly. I can't wait till my dear brother sees this. It was all his fault on why I'm against him. Mom and dad always favored him over me and I'm older than him but they decided making him Alpha and King was better then putting me as Alpha and King. It's all Edrick's fault.

"Ready than I'll ever be" she said smirking and we all headed out getting ready to attack. This is going to be a glorious day... Well for us it will be.

Edrick's PovWe were driving back home after we got frozen yogurt. We all talked and laughed but I couldn't get my mind off of Evangeline. She must be terrified. She must have given up on me by now. My chest squeezed in pain and I scrunched my face up knowing what was happening they were touching her again. We soon got home but everyone but yelling and screaming. I immediately got out and shifted fighting off some rouges and then I saw it. Evangeline with Derek and Zane walking from the woods with vampires. Zane gave me a smile showing off his fangs while Evangeline smirked thy shifted while the vampires attack some of my warriors. I growled loudly and went straight to Zane.

Evangeline go to the safe house! You'll be ok there! I yelled through our mind link to hear her laugh then shift attacking me. What? What did they do to her?

Evangeline? Evangeline! Stop! I yelled at her snarling making her step back and circle me snapping.

What did you do to her Zane? I demanded while Zane gave a wolfie chuckle making Evangeline make a snorting noise resembling a taunting huff.

She's one of us now Edrick. She wants power. She finally came to her senses he said making me snarl at him making Evangeline bark at me. I gave Zane one last glare until I looked over at me mate.

Evangeline it's me Edrick.... I'm your mate... Please snap out of it... I said whimpering at her and her eyes softened a little bit they became viscous again when Derek yelled remember at her then shifting attacking some of my members. Evangeline shook her head back and forth trying to come back to me. I guess she is commanding the rouges and vampires with her powers because she made them go on one side while whimpering.

Edrick.... T-tell you-r warriors to g-go on the other side-e she said I nodded and do so while she cracked a ripple in the ground capturing all the vampires and rouges putting fire in the pit of it. Derek and Zane where the only ones out. She looked at me then fell to the ground breathing heavily. I ran over to her licking her ear until her eyes opened again and snapped at me she looked over at the people she trapped and I knew she was going to u leash them again but then something amazing happened.

"Evangeline! Stop this! Now!" An angelic voice called we all looked up seeing the sky turn darker with the moon up glowing brightly. Selene... The Goddess of the Moon. I bowed down seeing her and so did everyone else having a deep connection and pride for her.

She was beautiful. She looked like she was in her late 20's even though she's been around for decades. Her hair flew like she was in water while her dark eyes glowed white she looked like Evangeline.

"Evangeline. Hunny. I didn't send you here to cause all of this. I sent you here to save everyone. And that's exactly what your going to do. You have a heart of gold and I expect you to act like it." she said lifting an exhausted Evangeline off the ground making her glow. She then had a spot black fur on her shaped like the moon.

"I love you my daughter. This is your destiny" Selene said then going away. Evangeline stood up proudly while her eyes glowed white just like Selene. She jerked her head towards Derek and Zane then the rouges and vampires. She arose from the ground levitating. She barked making a glow cascade down to them making Derek and Zane howl out in pain the the rouges whimper while the vampires hissed.

I command that you leave now and leave my pack alone. The vampires will be in peace with us werewolves and as for you rouges I want you all to stay away from packs and leave us alone and Derek and Zane leave and pray no one will ever see you cause if they do you'll have to deal with me! She barked and let them get past the hole in the ground making them run off whimpering filling the hole with water and sprouting a tree in the middle of the tiny space with flowers. She came back to the ground and shifted into a white gown with a ring on her middle finger. I shifted back running up to her hugging her. She giggled and wrapped me up in a big leaf covering me up.

"Edrick do you know what this is" she said feeling her ring. I looked at her and her eyes where white again. She was blind again. The prophecy..... She will have to sacrifice something she loves dearly to do all of this... I looked down at her and said no.

"This is my mother's ring... Selene... She has one just like it... It bonds us together" she said smiling.

"Evangeline..."

"I'm fine Edrick.... I knew I was going to lose my sight again... I knew it. It's fine" she said cupping my face wiping a stray tear. I let a sob out and wrapped my arms tightly around her embracing her.

"I love you so much"

"I love you too Edrick...." ***I hope you all liked this update!

Who knew Evangeline was going to lose her sight again?

Who thought Selene would make an entrance?

What are your all's feeling right now?

Chapter 24- Life's Great

E vangeline's PovI was sitting far away from Edrick in Jake's hospital room. They told me when I was taken he was put into a coma. So I wanted to come. It's the third week Ive been in here. The thing is with my sight I can see when I shift into my wolf. My mom gave me that she knows I loved seeing everything so she granted me that, which I am very thankful of.

"I wish he would wake up... Does he have an injury's on him?" I asked and Edrick hummed at me.

"He did but they all healed but when Derek scratched his side it was deep and his claws were covered in wolfsbane so it affected him more" Edrick said exhausted. I've been away from Edrick and all males. I remember what they did... They touched me and they.. They raped me.. The power I had to banish them that day is long gone and now I'm just a broken shell of my former self.

"Evangeline will you please tell me what happened?.. I could feel it through our mark but I want to know that your ok" he said making me look towards him with unshed tears.

"That's because I'm not ok!" I yelled sobbing putting my head into my hands crying. I felt arms wrap around me and I knew it was Edrick from the tingles but I was so terrified for someone especially a male to touch me so I yelled and screamed for him to let me go. He did and called Max and Sam. I smelt them in the room and they came closer wrapping me in their arms.

"Help me... Please... They are coming.. Please"

"Who's coming Eve?"

"Derek and Zane.... They are coming! Please help! Please!" I yelled pushing them away covering myself as much as I could.

"Edrick we need to call your friend to come help her... This has been going on for the whole 3 weeks she's been back." Max said and he growled and then I smelt an unfamiliar smell making me scream and kick more.

"No! Please don't! Don't take me! Please!"

"You all need to hold her down so I can help her" the old feminine voice said, it's that one elder. I think her name was Carrie?

"Elder Carrie! Please help me! They're coming! Please!" She sighed and started chanting something is Greek making me squirm feeling everyone's intense stares on me.

"What are you doing! Please help me!"

"Shush child, I'm taking the pain away. I'm not taking the memories I'm taking the way you felt and how you fear others when those disgusting men touched you" she said making me kick and scream.

"Please they are coming! You need to help me!" Soon she was done and I felt different. I felt all the pain and disgust of their hands on my body. I can't remember how I felt other than anger. Pure anger. I'll never officially recover from those awful days or be my former sled but I will be strong from now on and live my life because I know they won't come back.

"Evangeline? Are you ok?" Edrick said cupping my cheeks. I looked down towards his voice and smiled at him. I grabbed his neck and planted a passionate kiss on his lips.

"We will be leaving now" Elder Carrie said leaving the room with her scent along with Max and Sam's scent.

"I love you" I said and Edrick chuckled pecking my nose. That was our first kiss after I came back from my state.

"I love you too my queen" he said making me laugh while smiling at him.

"E-Evangeline?..." a rough voice said I got up stumbling over things over to Jake's bed I grabbed his arm I think and squeezed he took my hand squeezing it.

"You're blind?..." He said and I smiled at him looking towards where Edrick was.

"Get the doctor and my family" I said and he went out of the room while I smiled down at Jake.

"I'm here. I'm here" I said over again while he out his hand on my check probably wondering how I got like this again. I closed my eyes and leaned into his touch. He's back.

—5 months later—"Edrick! I swear to my mother Selene I will kill you for doing this to me!" I yelled at Edrick while we drove to the hospital because I was going into labor. Yes I'm pregnant. Yes heat hit me in the face. Yes Edrick and I made love and he also remarked me. If you are wondering why it didn't take long is because werewolf pregnancies last 3 months. And let me tell you this baby wants to come out now! I squeezed Edrick's hand hard making him whimper a little. Soon we were there and I was rushed into a room giving birth to our baby boy.

"Evangeline he's beautiful" Edrick said holding him. I smiled playing with my hands wanting to cry from happiness and sadness. I'm happy because I have a son a beautiful son and I'm sad because I can't see him. But soon I was shift and see him for myself.

"Can I hold him? You've been hogging him ever since he came out of my womb" I said laughing he laughed to and settled him in my arms. I smiled and put my hand on his stomach letting him grab my finger.

"Hello. I can to get your babies name" a human woman said walking in and I smiled warmly at my baby and over where the woman's send was coming from making her surprised I knew where she was.

"Theo. Theo Alexander Evans" I said and she hummed and wrote it down leaving.

"Welcome to our crazy work Theo" Edrick said making me laugh at him and shake my head, then I heard Theo giggle at me making me smile.

"I can already tell you're going to be a handful and a be a ladies man" I said rubbing his chubby stomach.

"He has my eyes and my mother's and fathers hair color brown" he said making me look towards him.

"Curly hair?" I said and he said yes making me giggle then our family started to come in but Jake got Theo first making them all pout. ***Another update! The next chapter will be the last one my magical sea unicorns! I loved writing this book and of course I had trouble from all the people saying stuff but I got through it with all you guys! I couldn't have done it with out you my magical sea unicorns!

You all can ask questions!

Chapter 25- My Ever After

E vangeline's PovI was in Theo's room cleaning up his toys when I heard someone walk in and pull me to them. From the tingles I knew it was Edrick. I sighed and turned over in his arms looking up at him smiling.

"S 'agapó agóri moró" I said to Theo then back at Edrick. I learned Greek over the past few weeks and because I'm the Moon Goddess' daughter it cane to me naturally.

"Hello" I said and he pecked my lips then his forehead on mine. I felt him go down and I was confused until he grabbed my hand and started speaking.

"Evangeline Meadows Rose. Will you stay with me forever. Stay by my side. Give me the privilege of impregnating you with more of my pups. Letting me wake up to you in my arms every morning. Let me worship you. Will you make me the happiest hybrid in the world and marry me?" He said making me cry into my hand.

Say yes you dummy! Say yes! Amber yelled at me making me nod my head frantically. I felt him slip the ring on my finger making me cry and wrap my arms around his neck kissing him hard.

"I love you so much Vasílissa mou" Edrick said resting his head on mine picking me up taking us to our bedroom.

"I love you O vasiliás mou" I said and we made love again.

—3 months later—It's time, oh lord. It's time. I walked back and forth with my wedding dress in my hands keeping me from tripping. Oh lord! Am I ready for this? Where is Theo?

"Hunny it's time come on" mom said and I walked over towards her voice and dad.

"Are you ready for this?" Dad said and I nodded I heard the music turn on and people stand when we walked in. I got mom to carry Theo so he could throw flowers. Sam is my maid of honor and Edrick's best man is Jake.

"He's crying" dad said making me laugh a little with unshed tears. I always promised myself when I got married if my husband to be didn't cry when he saw me I would leave.

"Take good care of her" dad said while handing me over to Edrick.

"I will sir. I I'll die first before I elf anything happen to her" he said making my dad grunt in approval.

"Hello everybody"

"Hello Selene"

"Dearly Beloved, we are gathered here today in the presence of these witnesses, to join Evangeline Rose and Edrick Evans in matrimony commended to be honorable among all; and therefore is not to be entered into lightly but reverently, passionately, lovingly and solemnly. Into this - these two persons present now come to be joined. If any person can show just cause why they may not be joined together - let them speak now or forever hold their peace" my mother Selene said and everyone was quiet. Then our vows came.

"Evangeline. I wanted to say that I love you and when I first met you it wasn't ideal" he said while laughing making everyone else laugh. "But I saw how stubborn and special you were and that just made me fall more in love with you. So I, Edrick Jace Evans, take you, Evangeline Meadows Rose, to be my lawfully wedded wife, to have and to hold, from this day forward, for better, for worse, for richer, for poorer, in sickness and in health, until death do us part" he said and I smiled at him then it was my turn.

"Edrick. I absolutely thought you were a psychopath when I first met you. I was terrified but I got to know you and thought of you as a really good friend and it became more than that. And we had a beautiful baby boy" I said hearing Theo make a baby noise making me laugh. "So following that I, Evangeline Meadows Rose, take you, Edrick Jace Evans, to be my lawfully wedded husband, to have and to hold, from this day forward, for better, for worse, for richer, for poorer, in sickness and in health, until death do us part" I said and he rubbed his hands over my knuckles.

"I now pronounce you husband and wife, you may kiss the groom" my mother said making me smirk.

"Wha-" Edrick was cut off by be grabbing his face and kissing him making everyone clap and my mother angelical laugh. Now off to the honeymoon!

—15 years later— "Theo can you go get your sisters?" I asked my 15 year old son. He nodded going upstairs getting May and Paige. Paige is 8 and May is 2. Paige is a spitting image of me, Theo is Edrick, and May is a mixture of both of us. They all are werewolves except for Paige and she has a tough time with her hunger but Edrick is helping her with it. She doesn't need blood all the time because she does have a werewolf gene but the vampire one takes over completely.

"Mommy! I drew you a rose!" Paige said handing me a piece of paper. I smiled and put my hand out and rested it on her cheek.

"It's beautiful baby" I said to her making her giggle and put it on the fridge while I made breakfast.

"Good morning" Edrick said pecking my lips and walking over to the girls.

"Daddy look what I made mommy!" Paige said and he laughed and told her it was beautiful. I heard May giggle at him making me smile.

"Do you need help mom?" Theo said and I nodded,"can you give me the milk my hands are kinda tied" I said mixing the eggs, putting the toast in the toaster, and cooking the bacon. I felt the jug hit my gently and I grabbed it from the air. Theo got to control the wind and Paige got earth while May got my bite but she is still to young to shift but we figured it out when she accidentally bit Paige's pet mouse making it turn to gold. I turned it back so Paige wouldn't get upset though.

"Breakfast is ready" I said and set the plates on the table sitting down and felt a kiss on my cheeks and forehead.

"Now May kiss mommy" Theo said to May is a baby voice and I puckered my lips up making May giggle and put a small kiss on my lips making me laugh at her. This is my happily ever after.